RECKONING
TEN SEASONS IN FIRE ISLAND PINES

A FICTIONALIZED MEMOIR

RECKONING
TEN SEASONS IN FIRE ISLAND PINES

A Fictionalized Memoir

MILES CIGOLLE

SUNSTONE
PRESS

SANTA FE

Sunstone books may be purchased for educational, business, or sales promotional use.
For information please write: Special Markets Department, Sunstone Press,
P.O. Box 2321, Santa Fe, New Mexico 87504-2321.
Printed on acid-free paper
∞
eBook: 978-1-61139-748-2

Library of Congress Cataloging-in-Publication Data

Names: Cigolle, Miles, author.
Title: Reckoning : ten seasons in Fire Island Pines / Miles Cigolle.
Description: Santa Fe, NM : Sunstone Press, [2024] | Summary: "The gay
    party scene on Fire Island Pines continued, even during the AIDS
    crisis"-- Provided by publisher.
Identifiers: LCCN 2024025609 | ISBN 9781632936738 (paperback) | ISBN
    9781611397482 (epub)
Subjects: LCSH: Cogille, Miles | Gay men--Biography. | Gay men--New York
    (State)--Fire Island Pines--20th century. | AIDS (Disease)--New York
    (State)--Fire Island Pines--20th century. | LCGFT: Autobiographies.
Classification: LCC HQ75.8.C586 A3 2024 | DDC
    306.7662092--dc23/eng/20240613
LC record available at https://lccn.loc.gov/2024025609

WWW.SUNSTONEPRESS.COM
SUNSTONE PRESS / POST OFFICE BOX 2321 / SANTA FE, NM 87504-2321 /USA
(505) 988-4418

FOR
MORTY NEWBURGH
IN LOVING MEMORY

PREFACE

This book is a fictionalized memoir based largely on real events and real people over a ten-year span near the end of the 20th century. It's a tale of longing, of celebration, of quiet introspection. Names of people and places are changed. If you weren't there, it may seem unbelievable, but that was the very nature of the Pines. It was a heightened world of bronzed men in Speedos strolling on the beach, of sweaty gym bods dancing shirtless in the Pines Pavilion until dawn, of horny musclemen searching for their next hookup in the Meat Rack under a full moon. The mourning doves at daybreak always made me sigh. During those years, AIDS was the uninvited guest who wouldn't go away. The Pines was where we grew up, where we found our community, where we broke down and bared our bravest hearts.

IN THE BEGINNING

BIRTH

I was a late bloomer. I didn't officially "come out" until my fourth year at Cornell. I was twenty-three. I clearly knew I was attracted to men long before that. Afterall, I was only five years old when I started paying close attention to the naked men in the shower room of my parent's pool club back in Albuquerque.

Once I discovered Morrie's, the only gay bar in Ithaca, it only took me a few months to hook up with Jim, a French Literature professor at nearby Wells College. Jim and I eventually moved to New York City where I lived for the next twenty-five years. Jim and I were considered a role-model gay couple—monogamous, domestic and artsy, who even spent Thanksgivings with my family in Providence, Rhode Island. We were respectable by all standards. Sure, and why not, we even had annual subscriptions to the New York City Ballet in Lincoln Center. Jim taught me to appreciate George Balanchine. The relationship lasted a good nine years, which back in those days was considered a small miracle. It was a wonderful loving relationship, but like most first-time pairings, it was doomed to failure. I was just a kid when we met in 1973—short on life experience, long on expectations. Jim was nine years older, of another generation completely. The generation that had cocktails before dinner. He was strictly Ivy League, haunted by too much guilt and shame. He wasn't even the least bit interested in gay porn. We watched the Gay Pride Parades from the sidewalk, rather than from the asphalt with our gay brothers in the street. Jim was just a little too uptight. Our limited sex life had become predictable, quite boring.

In our seventh year together Jim's Princeton buddy Gordon was passing through town and arranged a visit to The International Stud and its infamous backroom. Jim thought it would do me good. "Miles, go ahead, you'll have fun." I did indeed. That was the turning point. Monogamy was out, anonymous sex was in. The baths, the bookstore backroom, the J.O.

club, and always The Stud for the best blow jobs. Never a word about AIDS, the gay cancer. We were all in total denial. Jim and I broke up in 1982. I was thirty-one, single, in my prime and here I was about to be plunged into the wild New York City gay party scene. The music was loud; the men were intoxicating.

These were to be my golden years. It was supposed to be the best of times. In many ways it was just that. Within a year I met Abbey in Maneuvers, a slightly seedy leather bar in New York's Meat Packing District. He was my perfect dream lover, free of Jim's sexual hang-ups, complete with the leather jacket, faded 501s and the butch black moustache. He was both the leatherman I always secretly craved and the mushy Jewish mama's boy who needed nightly backrubs after sex so he could fall asleep in my arms. Abbey was my forever Prince Charming. Within three months he moved into my loft near City Hall. Abbey made me feel alive. We were inseparable; we did everything together. Once again friends said we were the dream gay couple.

In 1985 I was made Design Partner in a promising new Manhattan architectural firm in Tribeca. I felt accomplished with a few national design awards under my belt. Abbey and I moved into our new minimalist Midtown loft at Broadway and 29th Street which we created together. It was perfect for hosting dinner parties with Abbey's culinary skills on full display in the kitchen. We enjoyed the city's cultural riches with subscriptions to the Met, and best of all, Sunday afternoon Carnegie Hall piano recitals. We vacationed in Europe, Asia and the Caribbean. We occasionally blew off steam in raunchy backrooms of West Village leather bars. Abbey taught me how to let go and dance with the young gay Porto Rican kids in The Barn. With sex constantly on my brain, dancing was a healthy distraction. We really looked and acted like two West Village leather queens. All that overblown magic and fun was about to be seriously challenged.

WAKE-UP CALL

Oddly enough, looking back, it was in our darkest hour in the middle of the AIDS Crisis that the idea of Fire Island Pines first surfaced as an escape, pure and simple. It was 1985, long before the miracle AIDS cocktail drugs arrived a decade later. It was the Dark Ages. Abbey and I had been together for three years. Thankfully, we were both healthy. In those early years guys like us didn't get tested. It seemed pointless at the time. No one had the first clue what to do next if you were positive. Eat your vegetables; try an herbal diet.

Like most gay men living in New York City at the time, I was in denial. I was standing on the edge of a vast precipice. We all were, but few dared to look down. There were no AIDS drugs available at the time. Research was in its infancy. AIDS had only been officially recognized by the Centers for Disease Control and Prevention (CDC) in September 1982, and even then with much reluctance. President Reagan himself would not publicly acknowledge the epidemic until September 17, 1985, six months after Larry Kramer's AIDS play *The Normal Heart* premiered at The Public Theater. Abbey and I were in the audience along with Leonard Bernstein who broke down weeping at the final curtain. We all felt totally vulnerable. By the end of that year over 12,500 Americans had died, including Reagan's close friend Rock Hudson. With our community under siege, it felt natural to reconnect with our brothers. Fire Island was the obvious answer. During those frightening years, Fire Island Pines and Cherry Grove felt like safe havens.

We had visited both communities half a dozen times over several summers. They were simply out of this world in every way. "Gay Town USA." AIDS felt less terrifying there. We were surrounded by caring men who understood and shared our concerns. We perhaps aligned more easily with the butch Pines men, but our courageous feminine "sisters" in Cherry Grove also commanded our respect. Both communities complimented each other perfectly. The annual festive Pines Invasion said it all. We can all play together, even during the epidemic.

When early spring 1988 finally rolled around, I couldn't stop thinking about the Pines and all those friendly men. Maybe we should take a share in the Pines. I discussed it with Abbey. He also liked the idea. A new network of support. A new circle of friends. We started looking at the ads in the *New York Native*. One ad stood out immediately. "Looking for mature gay couples to share 4BR Japanese style FIP house. Pool. Nonsmokers only. Full shares only. Full season. $4,000 to $5,000 per bedroom."

When I called the number I was connected with a friendly guy named Murray, a co-owner of the Pines beach house at 124 Sunset Walk. He said Abbey and I could stop by his office after work anytime for an informal interview with himself and Ralph, the other co-owner. We thought it was a good sign that the owners were involved and would also be our housemates.

Of course, being an architect, I was immediately curious about the architecture of the house. Murray told me it was designed by an architect who had been an associate in I.M. Pei's office. When I mentioned I had worked in Pei's office, Murray sounded duly impressed. I asked him if he had a floorplan of the house. He sure did, from a Long Island Sunday newspaper supplement where the house was published in the sixties. We were terribly excited. It sounded too good to be true. We set up an appointment for the next week. Murray's law office was on Fifth Avenue next door to the New York City Public Library. Rothstein, Logan, Lincoln and Goldberg. Murray was the Goldberg.

NEW FAMILY

We liked Murray from the first handshake. Firm, but soft. He was short and skinny, always polite, always smiling. He handed me a copy of the magazine article on the beach house with color photos and a proper floorplan. I knew instantly we had hit a homerun. The house was perfect. Murray ushered us into the firm's comfortable conference room where the other co-owner Ralph was seated at the table. As we entered, Ralph rose to shake our hands. He was dressed entirely in a tailored black minimalist smoking jacket with matching trousers. I immediately thought of those Chinese dictators who seem to always stand silently still, cloaked in understated black elegance. Ralph was large to put it politely. He was actually obese. But he was extremely graceful. As he rose from the table, he appeared to float upward, effortlessly, like an enormous black dirigible. His tiny black shoes barely touched the floor. I thought of the ballet slippers on the male dancers at the New York City Ballet that I so admired. Ralph smiled and asked which of us was the architect. I confessed and complimented Ralph on his refined taste in beach houses. Murray had confided in me earlier that Ralph by himself had picked out the house on Sunset Walk which they ultimately bought together. The house's Japanese aura clearly spoke deeply to Ralph. It had been built by a straight couple who enjoyed the company of gay men. "Oh, they are so amusing at dinner parties!" The husband was a successful Long Island eye surgeon, filthy rich, the wife Janet was a local socialite who sponsored the annual Pines Art Shows at their even grander second Pines home, that one stark white overlooking the Great South Bay.

Ralph ran an art gallery in the city, Simmons International, based out of his modest Upper West Side apartment and he taught classes in the art of the painted finish. Things like small panel mosaics composed of crushed dyed eggshells. Ralph had real artistic talent. Murray deferred all aesthetic decisions to Ralph. I sensed Ralph and I would easily see eye-to-eye on delicate questions concerning the house appearance.

Abbey and I looked briefly over a neat list of house rules. Everything seemed reasonable and well thought out. It should be. Afterall, Murray was a successful lawyer. Abbey and I chatted briefly in private. There was no question, we both wanted in. The house was beautiful. Murray and Ralph looked like promising new friends. Based on the floorplan, I suggested we take the master bedroom overlooking the pool. Abbey agreed. We all shook hands and signed a few papers where we committed ourselves to a full share of the master bedroom for the long 6-month season running from mid-April to mid-October. $5,000.

On the way out, Murray gave each of us a warm hug. Later, we found out Murray is an only child, and like Abbey, he's Jewish and extremely close to his mother. Murray would become our future lawyer and a good friend for life. Ralph invited us to the next art opening at Simmons International. Of course, we said we would attend. We both knew this brief meeting marked the beginning of our new gay family.

GREAT EXPECTATIONS

There were still major unknowns. The largest question was who were our Pines housemates besides Murray and Ralph. Both co-owners were currently single and would each occupy small bedrooms on the main level for themselves and their personal guests. Abbey and I were in the master bedroom also on the main level. Downstairs were two additional bedrooms for a full-share couple or single guy. This arrangement left a downstairs bedroom open for invited guests. We would all take turns rotating the guest calendar. Guests were expected to eat with the housemates. The goal was to nurture an interesting core of gay men who would bond over the full season. Their guests would hopefully add variety to the core. Murray and Ralph had only rented out the house for the season once before. That experiment was a failure. It was run more like a hotel with strangers constantly coming and going. Our coming season was organized more like a commune made up of core family members and their occasional guests tossed in for interest. Abbey and I realized the potential risks, but welcomed the challenge.

Meanwhile, mid-April was still months away. Murray invited us out for the day in March to see the house. It was even more special than we had initially realized. It had traditional wooden Japanese post and beam construction applied rigorously throughout. It was constructed like a giant puzzle, logically put together piece-by-piece. The design formed a rectangular carpet laid over the landscape, made of a beautiful repeating open texture of 8'-4" square units. The entire house consisted of five by seven of these spatial units. A line of single unit courtyards weaved across the entire center of the plan, bringing light and greenery into the middle zone. It was brilliantly conceived and rigorously detailed in a Japanese tradition that celebrates human scale and a connection to nature. The house was truly an architectural masterpiece, more so than either Murray or Ralph fully realized.

We decided to host a dinner in our loft in the city for Murray and Ralph. We wanted them to see how we live. No clutter, clean, well-organized; let them see we are capable cooks in the kitchen. They both welcomed our participation in setting up the house. Murray asked me to track down a few dozen floor tiles that needed replacement. I suggested new window shades for the master bedroom. Abbey and I are serious lighting queens and volunteered to shop around and buy new fixtures with dimmers to professionally light the open beamed ceiling in the main living space. It would be a fun project. Murray and Ralph were delighted. Ralph could see we loved his beach house as much as he did.

We had our highest expectations for the grand social experiment. Friday April 16th would be our first day. Abbey and I left work at noon for the two-hour door-to-door trip. It included the Long Island Railroad to Sayville, then a taxi to the Sayville ferry landing, and the 20-minute crossing to the Pines Harbor. Of course, we were seated on the upper open deck with our brothers. The breeze on our faces felt good. The ferryboat was half full. Mostly homeowners opening up their houses for the season. Everyone looked extremely happy to be returning home after a long cold winter away from friends. Lots of long overdue hugs. As we entered the Pines harbor the ferry whistle blasted, announcing our arrival. We slid past the deck of the Blue Whale where high tea was in full swing with a dozen dancers. We could easily hear Donna Summer's new hit "Bad Girls" as overjoyed guys waved madly and blew us extravagant kisses. We had arrived.

SEASON ONE
1988

A QUEER'S
SANCTUARY

Murray and Ralph's Japanese Sunset Walk house was not a mere beach shack as you'd expect to find on a remote fragile sandbar like Fire Island. Rather, it was a sophisticated piece of serious architecture. It was cerebral, timeless and profoundly beautiful. Murray and Ralph probably suspected this since the house had roots in the high-brow architectural firm of I.M. Pei and Partners. But they never fully appreciated what they had purchased, nor did they take full responsibility that rightly came with ownership. That duty they would share with me since I had worked briefly in Pei's office. My opinion carried weight; but I had to tread lightly. At the end of the day, it wasn't my house, despite the fact I was sleeping in the master bedroom with Abbey.

It is telling to compare the beach architecture of the two adjacent gay communities—Cherry Grove and the Pines. Modern day Cherry Grove was first developed in the 20s. It was a motley collection of modest beach bungalows popular with gay artists, writers and successful hair dressers. They often had humorous, if slightly off-color names on driftwood boards nailed over their front doors: *Toolshed, Bottoms Up, Spank You Very Much, Mello Yellow* and *Dew Drop INN,* to name a few. Years later, gay designers, artists and lawyers settled next door in the more affluent Pines. They built modernist beach getaways designed by famous architects like Charles Gwathmey, Horace Gifford, Arthur Erickson and I.M. Pei. These elegant structures were high on sophisticated style and essential privacy, featuring huge pools and secluded decks for over-the-top parties. Famous gay designers and entrepreneurs like Halston, Calvin Klein, Jerry Hermann and David Geffen built enormous palaces that celebrated the pervasive spirit of gay liberation that followed the Stonewall Riots of 1969.

The Japanese style Sunset Walk house was equally sophisticated, but it was inspired by nature and domestic tranquility, not showy high-energy parties. To enter it was to step out of the Pines and immerse oneself in a state of Zen-like bliss, to enter a queer's sanctuary. The structure's lower level was sunk into the sand creating a solid foundation. Its broad sloped roof overhangs provided welcome shelter from the intense sun, plus soothing psychological comfort. The overgrown bamboo and American hollies surrounding the low-slung house on all sides created a dreamy world of dappled sunlight washing the wood decks. These largely uninhabited spaces abutted sliding glass doors, acting like spatial extensions of the modestly scaled interiors.

It was not grand like the famous Pines houses intended to impress with double-height ceilings and walls of glass. Rather, it was quiet, introverted and selfless, the perfect vessel to nurture close friendships, perhaps even new love. As the dappled sunlight entered the living room through full-height sliding glass doors, we'd often spend hours together, just talking on the sofas aimlessly, sharing with each other private matters of the heart. I'm sure Abbey and I weren't the first couple to make love on the wraparound sofa. A minimalist cast-iron fireplace was at the living room's center. It floated on a low brick plinth for logs. Tending the evening's log fire was always a welcome social event, the equivalent of a priest's offering of a bowl of golden apples in a Japanese shrine. The house was perfection itself.

TROUBLE

Our first Friday afternoon brought an unexpected jolt. Abbey and I had arrived early. We were delighted to find the front door open and the house apparently empty. We put a favorite piece of music on the stereo—Bach's Goldberg Variations performed by Glenn Gould. We had specifically brought out the CD for a special occasion on our first Pines weekend. We settled into the living room sofa. Abbey was in my arms. As usual, Abbey had me immediately fully aroused. Well this was certainly a special occasion. So we made passionate love on the living room sofa listening to Bach. It was pure heaven. Afterwards, I held Abbey in my arms, kissing his warm soft ears, making him laugh as we listened to the Bach. We were both extremely happy.

Suddenly, a door into the back of the house slams shut. We hear loud footsteps, a long silence, then more loud footsteps as we dress quickly. A tall blond man appears in the hallway leading into the living room. He hardly notices us. Within a few seconds he stops at the stereo, removes the Glenn Gould, puts on Swing Out Sister, turns up the volume, and vanishes as quickly as he came without speaking a single word. We're stunned. My heart is pounding. We're both furious. I walk over to the stereo, pull out the disc and restore the Bach. Within a minute the blond guy is back.

"Who changed my music?" "I did, you asshole! Who the hell are you?" "I'm Bradley. I'm Ralph's new boyfriend." "Well fuck you asshole. You are just the co-owner's latest trick. A freeloader, right? I thought so. Well, you don't get to pick the music on the living room stereo. We have a full share here at five thousand dollars. We pick the music. So get lost." I returned the Glenn Gould. Bradley says nothing, picks up his Swing Out Sister and disappears down the hall, his tail between his legs. I turn to Abbey. "What a flaming asshole." "Calm down Miles. Get over here. You're so sexy when you're upset." Abbey gives me a long hug; his hand soon inside my Levi's as he leads us into our bedroom closing the door. I start kissing him again. We spent the rest of the afternoon in bed making love. We were both on fire.

Thankfully, calm returns to the house that evening. Ralph says nothing about the CD fiasco. He cooks dinner for the five of us which will include Murray. Bradley keeps to himself cleaning the pool.

The three remaining housemates will arrive in the morning taking the two remaining bedrooms downstairs. This includes a couple, Donald and another Bradley. Donald is the editor of an important business journal. His twinkie boyfriend Bradley has an on-line gay travel business. A single geriatric psychiatrist named Trevor will take the other downstairs bedroom. I immediately want to meet him. I assume he will bring some gravitas to the house. That gives us eight full shares counting Ralph's Bradley. We think it's the perfect size. Given the immediate confusion with two guys named Bradley in the house, Ralph suggests calling the couple Donald and Bradley simply "The Darlings." Brilliant. Ralph introduces his new boyfriend Bradley to the housemates. Bradley and Ralph have only been together a month.

Murray grills the swordfish steaks. After dessert, he proposes we all go midnight dancing together at the Pines Pavilion. Great idea. We all have a ball getting down shirtless and sweaty. Ralph and his Bradley make a point of dancing with me and Abbey. Bradley buys us beers. He's really trying. He's a terrific dancer, much better than me, especially when Swing Out Sister comes up. He shows me how to move my hips. We share a good laugh and he gives me a warm hug. He's a very sexy guy. I can see why Ralph fell for him. He's an Alternative Medicine doctor, a quack in Abbey's book. Oh well, at least we will have one real doctor in the house.

We aren't in bed before three in the morning. At daybreak, just a few hours later, the mourning doves do their thing making a racket and I can't get back to sleep. I guess I'll have to pick up some good ear plugs. It's just mother nature asserting herself, reestablishing the natural order. The Pines is unnatural; that's for sure. I can understand why the Jesus freaks say we brought AIDS on ourselves. Maybe, but does that mean we all have to die? I don't know. I'm exhausted. I'm already falling in love with the Pines. Despite the CD fiasco, I love the place.

TREVOR

I woke up Saturday morning in Abbey's arms. It was nearly noon. The queen-size bed was too small and the clearstory window let in too much light. I was worried the room was unlivable. Abbey was unsympathetic. "You're in the Pines dummy. That's gay heaven. I'll get my baby some ear plugs and black-out eye shades. As for the small bed, I think it should improve our sex." As usual, Abbey was right.

I was eager to try out the outdoor shower next to the pool. It was in the shape of a giant conch shell open to the sky. I love being nude outdoors. It's so naughty. As a child I always loved showering outdoors or with the men in our pool club. I guess I'm an exhibitionist. It's a reaction to growing up as a Catholic prude. Abbey would say that was obvious. Anyway, the Sunset Walk outdoor shower was a ten.

The house was still half asleep. Abbey and I got dressed in tank tops and shorts. Murray handed us coffee cups in the small kitchen. He told us to get our butts on the back deck and welcome our new housemate Trevor. He had just arrived on the eleven o'clock ferry from the city.

Trevor was alone in the pool. He looked anxious. Despite that, he was really cute. A wrestler's trim body. His wet thick black hair was mussed the way Greek Gods are often portrayed in classical sculptures. He clearly worked out. With one hand, he was holding a small red swimmer's kickboard. It must have been a childhood treasure. He called up to us with a soft hesitant "Hi." His broad smile was adorable. I could see myself in him immediately. An awkward shy kid. We were distant brothers. I knew then we had a best friend for the summer and maybe much more. Everything would be all right. I felt wonderful.

We soon learned Trevor had recently split-up with his first-time boyfriend Joe. They broke up just a few days ago. Trevor decided to take the full share by himself at the last minute. As he told us this I could see the pain

25

in his face. It sounded awful. I wanted to hug him, to assure him things would be all right, but that seemed too forward as I hardly knew the guy. Abbey asked if he'd care to join us in a walk to the Pines Pantry for muffins for the house. "Absolutely, I'd love to." So that was how we met Trevor. He was a bit of a klutz like me. When he walked on the boardwalk to the Pantry he shuffled along at the rear of a line. He constantly used his hands to gesture and give emphasis to his speech. And what speech. Trevor was not just humorous, he was kind, wise and empathetic. It was easy to see the geriatric psychiatrist in him. In a house full of drama queens, Trevor was a welcome calm, the rocky coastline facing a stormy sea.

Trevor wasn't a cook. That critical house skill fell to Ralph and Abbey and to a lesser extent to me making the salads. Poor Trevor couldn't boil water for an egg. He confided "The kitchen is a dangerous place." So he rarely entered the kitchen at all. One Sunday morning Trevor was up early. Abbey made the coffee. I spread out the Sunday *New York Times* on the breakfast table. Trevor volunteered to toast the English muffins in the toaster oven. Simple, right? Not for Trevor. He loads the muffins, pulls down the lever. KA-BOOM! My God, what an explosion! Smoke, a flash of light. A total meltdown. The heating element exploded. Probably due to salt air getting into the heating elements. "See, the kitchen is a dangerous place."

We soon learned we had an ally when choosing the music on the living room stereo. When we pulled out our Glenn Gould Goldberg, Trevor lit up. Turns out he's a Bach freak just like us. Great! A welcome break from Bradley's Swing Out Sister and Tracy Chapman. The next weekend we brought out more Bach. Heinrich Schiff's Cello Suites and Richter's Well-tempered Clavier. Trevor could listen to Bach all alone in the living room for hours.

Trevor was always up for a shared adventure. Early on in the summer Trevor asked us if we'd be interested in having lunch in Cherry Grove at Top of the Bay. I said sure; we could walk through the infamous Meat Rack on the way. I'd been there a few times, mostly in the daylight and once under a full moon. That visit was the most incredible. The place was packed with guys. Everything looked silver in the moonlight. It was beautiful.

Trevor was completely silent the whole time we were in the Rack, as if we were in church. We passed a hot threesome really going at it. We stopped to watch. The participants didn't mind us in the least bit. In fact, I think our presence really turned them on. In his typical nonjudgmental fashion, Trevor announces the man in the middle is a friend. "He's a real pussycat once you get to know him. He's a statistician with a major pharmaceutical company."

Our morning house tour of the Grove was amusing. The men were all super friendly. One guy actually hinted at a foursome. Actually, they were more polite than the Pines men who are generally so full of themselves. But after a few hours, we'd had enough of the glitter and fluff and headed for the beach back to the butch Pines.

Along the way we ran into Murray and a man with a huge sunhat. Murray introduced everyone to his friend, the local landscape painter John Laub. John handed us invitations to a show of his latest paintings for sale starting next week. Maybe we'll purchase the small landscape on the postcard. It had a Japanese feel; perfect for our Pines bedroom. A souvenir of the summer. As John peeled off, Murray explained John has full blown AIDS. Years ago John and Murray were an item. Murray still loves John. John is clearly an inspiration; he just keeps going and going. Murray met up with more friends. He really does know everybody.

On the remainder of the walk back we started talking about the Meat Rack. Trevor asked to sit down at the water's edge. "I have a little confession for you both. I really like you two and I want to be honest with you from the start. I'm new to all this. I've only been in the Meat Rack a few times. Mostly at night so it's concealed. I met my first boyfriend Joe there. I always practice safe sex. I took the share at Sunset Walk to make friends with guys like you in the daylight rather than in silence in the dark."

Abbey and I hugged Trevor for what seemed a long time. We understood what Trevor was going through. We took turns talking about our relationships in the past. It felt good. Trevor is so easy to be around. Abbey shared stories of his times together with an older leather couple. It lasted for a year. That's all in the past now, long before Miles and AIDS arrived. I am way behind Abbey. I'm still drawn to the scene in the Rack, mostly as a voyeur. Abbey always does his best to keep me out of trouble.

Trevor took our hands forming a circle. "Let each of us pledge to look after each other with selfless love. Together we are stronger." We each took the simple pledge and hugged one more time. We walked back to the house in silence. I felt lucky to have met Trevor.

THE DARLINGS

When they first appeared late Saturday morning of our first weekend in the house, I thought it must be a joke. Ralph introduced them as "The Darlings." They were the most unlikely couple. Actually, their real names were Donald and Bradley, but the stage name "The Darlings" stuck. Donald was an old boyfriend of Murray's. They'd been together a few months several years ago and had remained good friends ever since. That relationship was easy to imagine. Both were professionals. Murray was a partner in a gay law firm. Donald was the editor of an important financial newspaper.

Donald and Bradley were another matter altogether. Bradley was your classic gay twinkie, an airhead, always smiling like he was on drugs, with absolutely nothing to say other than "Hi guys!" Bradley was half Donald's age and ran an on-line gay travel business. It didn't list sites to visit, accommodations or restaurants as in a normal travel guide, rather it mainly told you where gay men looking for sex could hook up with similarly inclined gay men anywhere across the globe. Bradley "researched" each entry personally providing maps and helpful tips. His entries for New York City, Marrakesh and London were particularly lengthy and colorful. Besides the travel thing, Bradley mostly spent all his free time in the Chelsea Gym, or more precisely, in the gym's steam room fooling around.

Clearly Bradley was Donald's boy toy. He had a nice body, a reflection of his fortunate youth. They had taken the full share for the slightly larger downstairs bedroom adjacent to Trevor's. They only came out every other weekend since Donald always had pressing deadlines. Being downstairs himself, Trevor saw the most of them, even though he found Donald pretentious and ill-informed when it came to modern psychiatry. Plus Trevor has always been a serious devotee of the British Royals and found Donald's phony British accent disrespectful and deeply offensive.

Trevor confided to Abbey and me, that The Darlings could easily be an S&M couple. The walls at 124 Sunset Walk were paper thin. You could easily hear sharp slaps and long moans through the walls. Trevor was even certain Donald was the top. The poor guys had no privacy. But Trevor was absolutely on the mark about sound in the house. Abbey and I could similarly hear Ralph and Bradley going at it in threesomes with guys Bradley picked up in the harbor in the wee hours. When they were done, they'd sneak out the back door into the night. Never a word come morning. It truly was hard to get a good night's rest.

The downstairs conveniently had its own separate entrance, so anyone sleeping there could come and go unnoticed. We were all night owls. My own midnight visits to the Meat Rack were usually with Abbey and we simply used the front door. We figured everybody must have figured it out by our second weekend so why pretend. One bright full moon, Abbey and I ran into Bradley Darling by himself wandering in the Rack. Without missing a beat he greeted us with his usual innocent smile. "Hi guys," as if we were headed to Baskin Robins for an ice cream cone.

Abbey and I were always pleased when Donald returned from his travels for work. He'd tell hysterical stories in the living room for hours, mostly sex adventures from his foreign travels, like the horny conductor who fucked him in an empty first-class compartment or better yet with the cute bell hops in fancy European hotels. Tight elevator compartments were often the perfect setting for a quickie. Donald always said the more fantastic the situation, the better the payoff. Once in an extremely long tunnel in the Swiss Alps, Donald was screwed in the dark by a very knowledgeable conductor. As Donald relived the story, getting all excited, he described the great length of the tunnel with outspread hands. Then he got carried away demonstrating the conductor's athletic sex performance. Donald's tight fist smashed into Ralph's crystal flower vase on the coffee table. It shattered into a hundred pieces as it ricocheted off a wall. Donald had us all rolling on the floor. I was never quite sure where fantasy and reality parted in Donald's stories. They were all so naughty.

Somehow The Darlings' charm excused them from house chores. Maybe it was their bi-weekly schedule that always turned them into new arrivals, fresh with colorful stories. Afterall, it was the Pines. We wanted to have fun, to be entertained, to try something new, something more intense. AIDS had no place here. It was simply not on our dance cards. It was banished for the season. It will surely still be there when we return to the harsh unforgiving city at the end of summer. That will be our reckoning. But for now, we're in the Pines, our private world, surrounded by exquisitely beautiful men, all eager to fly, all eager to sample the exotic fruits of desire.

Donald noticed I was always giving him the once over around the pool. He favored boxer swimming trunks, which on his tall lanky body looked awfully sexy. So one quiet afternoon when just he and I were swimming, I retreated to the outdoor shower, dropped my Speedos, and waited patiently. Sure enough, Donald showed up smiling. "May I join you?" "It's about time." Donald is an English gentleman. He let me go first.

All this intense extracurricular activity went on all summer long without any acknowledgment at all. Not a single word. Of course, we all sensed what was actually going on right under our noses, but we all felt entitled to a silent pass, a "Get Out of Jail Card." Each of us deserved that, right? We'd earned it at all those funerals accompanied by tears, at every memorial service. But late at night as we slept in our beds we knew we were fooling ourselves. Bradley's gay travel guides were missing the maps to the queer cemeteries. We were all fooling ourselves.

WHITE LINES

Early in the season two pint-size cans of white house paint and a pair of paint brushes appeared on the boardwalk at the entry into 124 Sunset Walk. When Abbey spotted them he noticed the same arrangement at the neighbors across from us. Murray explained it was a Pines tradition. Every spring the Pines Property Owners Association supplies the paint and brushes. Each house is responsible for painting a two-inch-wide white stripe at the outer edge of the boardwalk as it crosses the property. It's a safety issue. There are no street lights in the Pines. At night it can get pitch black. The upside means the stars are fantastic, the downside is guys walk off the boardwalk into the bushes and twist a leg. We couldn't have that.

Abbey and I volunteered to paint the white line. We wanted it done right since we personally took great pride in our house. Some houses end up with sloppy jobs that look like some drunkard did it. Murray was pleased we took charge. Abbey asked me to do it since he knows I'm super-anal. No problem, I'm an architect; it came out perfectly, nice and straight. Ralph approved and as a thank you asked us what we wanted him to cook for dinner. That was an easy decision. Abbey asked for a favorite dish we'd had in Venice, vitello tonnato, veal with a creamed tuna sauce with giant capers. It's a ton of work, but Ralph didn't mind and accepted the challenge.

While I was on the boardwalk happily painting away, our neighbor directly across from us appeared. He was about to do the same thing and introduced himself. His name was Stan, about the same age as Abbey and me. He was dressed Pines casual, shirtless in running shorts. He had a very nice body. He was super friendly. We joked about my white line. "You definitely get the prize for the straightest line Miles. Now that's a straight line!" When Abbey appeared to say hello, Stan invited us over sometime to meet his lover George. Stan suggested getting together on Sunday since George is busy on Saturdays. He owns a pool cleaning business and Saturdays are always the craziest. Abbey said great, he's always up for new friends. Stan said he'd prepare a light lunch, nothing fancy. We could meet their baby Betsy, a basset hound sweetheart. No problem, we love dogs. Parting company, Stan said to wear our Speedos on Sunday so we could enjoy a long soak in their hot tub. He said George will insist on it.

The next day, Sunday, we were headed to Stan and George's for lunch. Big schlep; it's just across the boardwalk. Abbey loves basset hounds, so he was all excited to meet Betsy in her home. We'd actually seen her in the Pines harbor. It turns out Stan owns a small speed boat which he parks in the Pines harbor. Betsy often naps in the rear of the boat stretched out in the sun on cushions. She always welcomes attention from the guys strolling past. Abbey loves to stop to pet her. So on Sunday, when Stan opened the door to his house on Sunset, Betsy immediately recognized Abbey and jumped up to welcome her old friend.

Lunch was simple. Stan and George obviously aren't into cooking. But soon we discovered they are really into casual sex. Stan soon retired to the hot tub and invited us in. It was a deluxe model. Of course, George is in the pool business. Stan and George much prefer a hot tub to a pool. I immediately see why as Stan pulls off his swim suit to show off his hard dick. I'm not surprised. I thought this might happen. Stan is apparently interested in me. He starts playing footsie with my basket under the water. Things take off from there. Hot tub sex is a new experience for me. It was really "hot" in the other sense.

Afterwards, we talked in the tub for an hour. We certainly had made new friends. Stan invited us out on his boat for the following Sunday. Maybe lunch afterwards with some more fun in the hot tub. I told Stan once was terrific, but I didn't want to turn it into a Sunday routine. We valued our new friendship too much. Stan was great. He agreed to cool it with the sex and just enjoy each other's company. Stan gave me a warm hug and that was that. Abbey and I still visit Sundays. We bring the sandwiches. They supply the pooch. We even got together in the winter at their place in Woodstock. Stan gave me great advise when I had financial difficulties in my partnership. He was like a missing Dad.

HOUSE MOTHER

Every Pines house has a house mother. She emerges slowly, but eventually it is obvious who bears the title. That first summer, Ralph was our house mother. He maintained the domestic order, resolved conflicts, took the lead in all discussions of house aesthetics and most importantly oversaw everything in the kitchen while wearing his French apron. Ralph was our Julia Child. While others volunteered shopping and cooking dinners, it was always under Ralph's watchful supervision. Once when Abbey and I volunteered to prepare a fish steak dinner with baked potatoes and steamed broccoli, Ralph spotted the broccoli stems in the kitchen garbage. "Oh my God! Who threw out the broccoli stems?" They were apparently an essential ingredient in Ralph's Coq au Vin planned for the following night. Ralph made sure I was publicly humiliated. At dinner he announced to all that I had tossed perfectly good broccoli stems into the kitchen garbage. "He's such a control queen." That was his thank you for our preparing the night's dinner.

Actually, the truth is, both Ralph and I were major control queens, Ralph in the kitchen and me in the living room. That wasn't always a bad thing. We ate extremely well and the lighting in the living room was always perfect. A good example of Ralph's leadership was on a chilly stormy Friday evening after work very early in the season. The rain was heavy, the wind was constant. Our ferry boat really should have turned back. Ralph, Trevor and Donald were also on the same ferry with Abbey and me. Several obnoxious lesbians with large dogs kept opening the cabin door letting in the rain. They were so butch.

Our ferry crossing was unusually rough. The boat was packed full of provisions to open up houses, not to mention the soaked dogs eager to get off the ferry. As we approached the mouth of the Pines Harbor, a rogue wave pushed the ferry onto a sand bar. We were stuck. Our rescue took the Harbor

Master and the Pines Fire Department over three hours to arrange. We had to be transferred to smaller boats, in groups of six, across hastily arranged wood planks. By the time we all touched down on the boardwalk, the Pines Pantry was long closed. As Ralph opened the front door at 124 Sunset Walk, we sensed impending disaster. The roof appeared fine, but the kitchen was bare. The refrigerator was empty, the cupboards held zip except for some funky condiments and dried spices. Ralph grabbed his apron and went to work.

We usually had dinner on the spacious screened-in porch which could easily accommodate twelve. Given that the remnants of the storm were still overhead, that dining option was ruled out. Ralph took charge and announced we'd be eating inside at the breakfast table. Like a General, Ralph called out assignments to his troops. The Darlings would tend a fire in the living room and light candles throughout the house since a power failure was likely. Murray would check all the windows and doors for leaks. Miles would do his magic setting the smaller breakfast table for eight, up from the normal six. Abbey was recruited as Ralph's assistant chef. Trevor would report shortly for dish washing duty. Bradley would oversee the stereo music making sure his selections pleased everyone. With all the bases covered, Ralph placed all the available cooking ingredients on the kitchen counter. It was pretty pathetic, especially when compared to the usual mountain of indulgent excess. We only turned up one can of tuna, a box of unopened pasta shells, a bottle of calamata olives, pinion nuts, grapefruit juice, one onion and a half-used tub of butter. A warm six-pack of beer in the back of the pantry was immediately placed in the empty freezer. Plus, a couple of small open popper bottles were in the frig crisper drawer. The wine rack was empty, but the dry spice rack was crammed full with every spice imaginable. To make matters worse, we were all starving. Bradley half-jokingly suggested we get out the popper bottles and strip down for an orgy in the living room to take our minds off the storm. Ralph ruled from the kitchen "No way!" and announced that dinner would be on the table in just one hour. Indeed it was, with the table set for eight and the candles lit. Ralph pulled off a culinary triumph. Afterwards, he named the dish "Ralph's Stormy Pasta." The eight of us huddled around the small table. That shared adventure on a stormy night, brought us together for the first time. It was a house highpoint, frequently recalled with pride to our dinner guests.

That summer Ralph would prepare numerous complex dishes including Beef Bourguignon and an over-the-top Indian feast. For that spectacular Indian dinner Ralph appeared dressed in full Indian costume including a sexy

V neck long-sleeve Mao Collar Cha cabana with a vintage white head turban. The entire evening Ralph never broke his thick Indian accent.

Ralph was very sensitive to his hefty girth. He walked slowly with great control and grace, especially around the pool apron. It was his personal stage. He'd gladly demonstrate his superiority in diving. He pierced the water's taut surface without making a single splash. Afterwards, he enjoyed swimming across the pool with a stem glass full of wine, traversing the pool perfectly, never spilling a drop, as if he was a silent hovercraft.

Apparently, Ralph's carefully studied grace was insufficient for his demanding boyfriend Bradley. Bradley was skinny and the narcissist inside him required an equally skinny lover. By the time the season arrived, Bradley had already enrolled poor Ralph in his Nazi starvation diet, "a cup of clear broth and a leafy green salad." Bradley was unrelenting. The diet was totally inflexible. Once he'd achieved his Machiavellian goal of Ralph shedding a hundred pounds, he demanded Ralph submit to a complete tummy tuck to remove the unsightly hanging flesh. Ralph endured it all silently. Anything to be able to say he had an attractive boyfriend, that he finally fit into the Pines, that he owned not just a beautiful beach house, but the sexy hot lover that came with it. It was time to leave the safety of his hidden fenced-in pool and stroll the open beach unashamed like those mindless airheads, those Pines Boys parading the beach in their skimpy Speedos. Poor Ralph would try anything once.

Abbey and I felt cheated. When we first met Ralph at our interview, before Bradley arrived on the scene, we thought we'd found an interesting new friend for life, someone we could share our love of art with, especially a love of all things Japanese. When we saw his wood block prints hanging on the walls at Sunset Walk we were impressed. Ralph was a gifted gay artist. He was always busy creating something: a mosaic from dyed crushed eggshells, an exquisite flower arrangement, an elaborate dinner party with costumes, a delicate woodblock print of the Pines boardwalk over the dunes. When Bradley arrived, Ralph's outgoing personality slowly receded, his colorful creative genius slowly faded away. Bradley demanded full attention during sex. No wonder he arranged for threesomes with Ralph and himself, using hired Porto Rican boys he'd picked up in the harbor. He could pay for kinky sex with strangers, making up for Ralph's limp performance. He humiliated Ralph in the process.

Abbey and I loved our misunderstood house mother Ralph. She was a saint amongst sinners. Once in late March, before the house on Sunset Walk officially opened, Abbey and I invited Ralph over to our loft in the city for dinner. We were eager to know our new housemate. This was all pre-Bradley. When I opened the front door, there was Ralph, dressed in his signature all-black uniform, holding the largest pot of flowering pink peonies I'd ever seen. It was stunning. It was also the only show of color in our stark white minimalist loft. It stood out like a sore thumb. Ralph knew immediately he'd made an aesthetic blunder. He blushed. We rescued him immediately, taking the enormous pot and placing it on a Japanese platter on the long, low white bookcase in the middle of the space, "Just what we really needed Ralph, a splash of color. Thank you so much. How did you know peonies were our favorite flower?" Ralph gave Abbey and me a long hug. Ralph looked around at the spartan loft and mumbled, "I don't know how they do it."

THE PAST

The past follows us like a faithful dog. It stays next to us whether we want it to or not. Bobby was still at my side. He was my first crush from the third grade at Mark Twain Elementary. That was long ago, before Fire Island, before Abbey, before Jim. Bobby held my hand on the school playground during recess, just the two of us, so content just humming mindlessly. Together we felt safe, free of the monster, the playground bully Doug. We held hands walking together around the playground perimeter in the shade of the giant cottonwoods. The summer thunderstorm came up suddenly, as they do in Albuquerque, with enormous raindrops washing our faces. I dared to touch Bobby's wet face. He smiled and kissed me on the cheek. I carry that tender kiss with me still, even here on Fire Island. It's with all the young men I meet here in the Pines, who smile at me when we pass on the boardwalks, who look at me longingly in the Meat Rack. They are still innocent boys, boys just like my Bobby, who never questioned love, but grabbed it when it was offered suddenly in a summer's thunderstorm. Love took hold of us violently, cracking open suddenly like a bolt of lightning.

It wasn't long before ugly rumors surfaced concerning 124 Sunset. Our beloved beach house, that we all found so perfectly magical, had a troubled past, a past Murray and Ralph never discussed with us. The *New York Native* ad which Murray and Ralph placed last winter didn't mention these rumors from the past. The season that preceded ours in the house was pretty wild. The Japanese style house was run like a hotel or perhaps more like a gay brothel with housemates and their tricks checking in and out at all hours. It was soon known as the Pines newest party house with plenty of drugs and sex. Abbey and I were surprised, secretly amused, as we imagined Murray and Ralph playing slightly different roles. Donald was there also. He'd remained a close friend of Murray's after their summer affair years ago. He spent plenty of time at 124 Sunset that season. He liked the continuous pot. On a long beach walk to Water Island during our first weekend together, Donald told us the whole backstory.

Back then Ralph was busy making up for lost time. He wanted to throw a notorious house party to show off his new beach house and his new trim waistline. Afterall, it was Murray and Ralph's first season as homeowners and they wanted to be noticed. Ralph carefully chose the theme, Bastille Day, the 14th of July. It appealed to his love of spectacle and all things French. Ralph dressed up as Marie Antoinette in an enormous gown with a white beehive wig. The pool was dyed red, complete with half a dozen floating severed heads. A guillotine graced the pool deck and guests lined up for mock executions. As the blade fell across a mirrored neck another head fell into the water with a splash of red dye. The crowd cheered wildly and demanded more. Ralph's Marie Antoinette was not to be spared, just as in the history books. Her torn dress and smashed bun of white hair ended up in the pool with half a dozen naked guys. It was generally terribly vulgar and silly, a display of complete debauchery, but it was judged a resounding success by the Pines twinkies. Ralph was pleased. The only downside was the bored drunken mob who trashed the house and used the huge living room sofa for an open-house orgy. Murray was most-definitely not pleased. He blamed Ralph completely. But anyone could see it coming. It was all to be expected.

The party left a sour taste in Murray's mouth. He started referring to it as "Ralph's French Orgy." The following weekend Murray came to me noticeably agitated. I'd never seen Murray upset, so I was concerned. Murray wanted my professional opinion. At the Bastille Day party last week a drunken guest fell off the back deck landing on Ralph's prize rhododendrons. Thankfully, he wasn't hurt. The prize rhododendrons were another story. Murray's litigious side immediately saw trouble. He could see himself getting dragged into an expensive lawsuit. He wanted me to design handrails for the decks. It sounded so simple, but it was a nightmare. Everything in the house design hugged the ground. It was a composition of horizontals. To add handrails, with their inevitable vertical supports, would violate a core principle of the design. I explained all this architectural gobbledygook to Murray as delicately as possible. He was unpleased with me. I felt trapped in a corner. As a compromise, I simply suggested the addition of low saucer-like flower pots with colorful low flowering plants strategically placed around the deck edges. This should subconsciously create a visual barrier that complimented the Japanese style of the house. Ralph applauded the idea. "Brilliant Miles!"

After seeing a couple of sample pots in place from the Pines Nursery, Murray came around. Thank God, an aesthetic catastrophe was averted.

Later on in the same summer, pure greed almost did in 124 Sunset altogether. It was the weekend of the GMHC Morning Party which attracts some three thousand men to the Pines from across the globe. Houseowners gladly vacate their houses and turn into greedy realtors overnight, renting their houses out at outrageous rates. Murray and Ralph saw dollar signs. So, no surprise, they rented the house out to a dozen Brazilian airheads for an outrageous sum.

Surveying the damage the following weekend, Ralph concluded that the unsupervised house rental idea was a huge mistake. Never again. The Brazilians left behind a wake of trash, used condoms, and cigarette burns on the white sectional wrap-around sofa. Even floor tiles were burned. Luckily the house wasn't set on fire. Murray secured their five thousand dollars security deposit in full, uncontested, no questions asked. When Abbey and I learned the details, we were stunned. Unfortunately, this behavior is not uncommon in the Pines, where money talks and simple greed rules. There is too much money, too many drugs and too little consideration for others and the fragile environment of the Pines.

There were other voices from the past, less strident ones, that entered 124 Sunset. They walked through locked doors and mingled between us; old lovers and distant friends. They sat across from us at the empty morning breakfast table, lounging in deck chairs as we napped around the pool, cuddling naked next to us in our beds, making passionate love to us in the shower. My first crush Bobby was there as well, still faithfully holding my hand, as we walked along the pristine beach still humming softly.

Early one Saturday morning the house phone rang. The lonely ring dared to break the empty silence. The panicked call was for Trevor. One of his hospitalized mental patients had escaped a facility due to the skeletal nursing staff on duty over the weekend. Trevor was accustomed to such crises, but the rest of us were not. The blunt news was deeply disturbing. I put down the *New York Times*. Suddenly, no one was hungry. Bradley, who always felt inferior around Trevor, who after all was a real doctor, not a quack, took the opportunity to torment Trevor with cruel jokes about shock therapy. Bradley only made the awkward situation that much worse.

We too were living on the edge, like Trevor's patient, with the uncertainty of AIDS staring us in the face. The Pines was a distant shore full of dead-end illusions, that and friendly ghosts. We too had escaped from a cold judgmental world that didn't understand us. We were searching for our Bobby. That night I held Abbey more tightly than ever. I knew then I was blessed.

BOB

Bob was my best friend. We met at Cornell and worked together at the Manhattan architectural firm Skidmore, Owings and Merrill (SOM). Abbey and I invited Bob and his lover Dave out to 124 Sunset as our first guests of the season. Bob and Dave were like the two middle-aged men in the classic movie *The Odd Couple*. Bob was definitely Jack Lemmon and Dave was surely Walter Matthau. Dave was cheap, cranky and critical, Bob was just the opposite—generous, fun and relaxed. It was to be their first trip to the Pines. Bob mainly wanted to check out the Meat Rack. He'd heard all about it. He was well versed in au natural queer sex since he and Dave lived on Central Park West directly across from the infamous Ramble. I loved to hear Bob tell his elaborate tales of steamy late-night sex in the bushes. Bob is so friendly and relaxed. When Dave was away on business trips for the Swiss bank, Bob would sometimes invite cute guys back to the apartment after sex to share a couple of beers together, trade life stories, getting to know each other a bit. He'd make new friends for life. In contrast, Dave was a judgmental prude, forever giving poor Bob a hard time. Bob had AIDS and recently went on full disability. You'd think Dave would cut poor Bob some slack. No such luck. I wanted to invite just Bob out to the Pines to have some fun away from his team of doctors, away from nurses and hospitals. I was secretly annoyed when Dave announced he'd be coming along as well.

Meanwhile, Trevor had taken off the entire week at 124 Sunset before we arrived. It was his first gay vacation. He was having a ball. He met someone special in the Rack. I want to meet him. His name is Beau. Trevor looked fantastic. He wanted to surprise his housemates by preparing his first and last Pines dinner. Well not exactly prepare, more like transport. Trevor made a special trip into the city to *Junoon* for an extraordinary Indian feast. He really got carried away carrying bags and bags of Indian dishes back to the Pines. It was unbelievable. It was really sweet since Trevor can't boil water. When we opened the door at 124 Sunset, Trevor welcomed us in with a delicious fresh fruit drink heavily spiked with rum. Indian music was on the stereo and several colorful beach umbrellas were suspended from the cathedral ceiling. Ralph wore his sari and turban. Bob and Dave were stunned. Abbey played along with Trevor and Ralph and just told his guests this was a typical Friday dinner at 124 Sunset. "Relax, you're in the Pines!"

That's about the time Bob vanished for an hour. When he finally showed up after a quick outdoor shower he looked his best in months. He winked at me and grinned an enormous smile. I understood precisely and gave Bob a long hug. I love Bob.

Trevor's Indian feast was a homerun, a personal triumph. It concluded with a refreshing dessert that was his own creation—frozen seedless grapes with lemon sorbet. Trevor received a resounding standing ovation from all, complete with hoots, hollers and blown kisses. Trevor started crying. I hugged him. I was so proud of him. Bob and Dave were handed a special "Welcome to the Pines" present, a box of Trojan Bareskin Condoms. It was an evening to remember forever.

After dinner Abbey and I proposed a short beach stroll under the full moon. Dave declined; he was too exhausted. Bob lit up; he loved the idea. On the beach walk headed to Cherry Grove, Bob thanked us profusely for the weekend invitation. He's at an impasse in his never-ending AIDS treatment and doesn't know what to do next. Abbey told him to call him first thing on Monday morning to get the name of the best AIDS doc. Abbey hugged Bob. "You're not alone Buddy. Keep up the good fight; we love you."

Where the beach meets the Rack we stopped. I told Bob I had something to show him. I led the way under the towering holly trees. All the twisted branches were silver in the moonlight. It was extremely beautiful, the vision of heaven itself. I walked on and turned where the ground dropped off and several large tree trunks had fallen, This was the spot I was looking for. It was brightly lit in the moonlight. You could make out half a dozen bodies moving slowly, silver torsos, silver bald heads, silver buttocks. It was a maze of men's silver bodies intertwined. It was very quiet. No one spoke, but I could hear heavy breathing, soft moans, occasional sharp slaps. We stood frozen and watched in silence for a very long time. It was extremely moving. Bob started to cry as I held him. Bob turned and spoke first. "Thank you Miles. Let's go back to the house. This has been one of the most special nights of my life." "Thank you Bob for coming. You know I love you like my brother."

The next morning the house was fast asleep when Abbey made the coffee. I pulled the *New York Times* out of its plastic sleeve and spread it out on the breakfast table. We hardly spoke. Abbey suddenly interrupted the silence and thanked me for the moonlit tour of the Rack last night. I told him it was my gift to Bob. "Bob is a dreamer. He needs to see the raw beauty of men loving men. He needs that in order to dream of the heaven that surely awaits him." Abbey started crying and hugged me.

An hour later, Ralph told us he'd seen Bob alone in the harbor, walking to the dock for the seaplane. They waved across the harbor. The distance was much too far for the delicate conversation in front of them. Ralph waved instead and blew Bob a kiss. Bob did the same in return. Turning up his leather jacket collar, Bob handed the pilot his gym bag and pulled himself onboard. The engine quickly gained speed as it slowly pulled away from the slim dock. The glass was too tinted to see the figures inside. Ralph waved anyway. He stood frozen, out of respect, until the plane took off, headed back to noisy Manhattan.

THE QUACK

Abbey and I felt more than a little deceived by Ralph and Murray when Ralph's new boyfriend Bradley appeared out of the blue. His name never came up in our interview. They'd only been together for a month before the house officially opened and it was soon obvious he didn't fit in. It wasn't just his disdain for opera and classical music in general, or his pattern of bringing young boys back to the house for sex, or his baiting Trevor because he was a real psychiatrist, as if Bradley was a real doctor himself. Plus, Abbey had figured out Bradley never really paid for his full share like the rest of us. It slipped out in conversation. It was considered a wedding gift from Ralph. It was Ralph's little secret. So on top of everything else Ralph's Bradley was a freeloader.

I also resented his misinformed influence on Ralph concerning the care of the house. One Sunday morning Ralph and Bradley were down on their knees painting the boards of the front deck with house paint. The dove gray boards were weathered, but with a subtle patina of moss and paint stain that was most flattering in the dappled light. I would never recommend opaque house paint for such a delicate Japanese-inspired structure, but rather transparent stain which protects wood while imparting a delicate finish. I was horrified. They had already painted a large area and the contrast was immediately apparent to anyone with eyesight. I protested loudly. Bradley told me to mind my own business. Ralph looked on in nervous silence. When I pressed Murray, he turned to Ralph and Bradley and suggested they stop painting for a month and see how the deck looks once the paint had a chance to cure. It remained untouched for the rest of the season. It was never discussed again. I blamed Bradley for the whole ugly episode. His impatient, controlling personality were to blame. No one ever reigned him in.

Bradley was the kind of gay man we generally avoided. We were professionals: a doctor, a lawyer, an architect, a banker. What was Bradley?

A disco queen, a DJ, a drug dealer, a hustler, an Alternative Medicine Man, a shyster. He looked like trouble. That was the last thing we wanted at 124 Sunset Walk. We could easily imagine police knocking at the door, Bradley in handcuffs, dogs searching the house for drugs. Were we overreacting? Perhaps. But Bradley made the rest of us nervous. He was a quack.

The label fit him. Ralph's boyfriend Bradley was a quack. He called himself an Alternative Medicine Doctor, but what did that mean? Voodoo medicine at best. I'll give you an example.

One quiet morning at 124 Sunset, before the paint episode, we had an even more upsetting display of Bradley's behavior. Abbey had volunteered to do the grocery shopping for dinner in the Pines Pantry. I decided to grab the open window of free time to work on my tan line. I headed to the beach in my favorite Speedos and flip flops for a short sun bath. 124 Sunset is a short walk to the beach. On the way, I had an accident on the boardwalk. In a hurry I stepped too hard on a split board, it snapped in two, and my leg fell through the hole to the sand a foot below. In the process, I'd cut myself just below the knee. I was bleeding badly. I rushed back to the house all upset. Bradley was in the living room listening to his Tracy Chapman on his headphones. He saw my bloody leg and leapt into action. I was to be his first patient in the house. Since Abbey was still out shopping, I nervously resigned myself to the awkward situation. I knew Abbey would be upset with me, but I was trapped. Bradley sat me on a towel on the living room sofa and disappeared into the kitchen. He soon returned holding a large dinner knife placing the broad side directly on the wound applying pressure as he rocked the knife side to side. The knife was extremely cold, apparently straight out of an ice pack. This all seemed most peculiar. I was most uncomfortable, but I didn't know what to say. After ten minutes, Bradley removed the knife and placed four bandages across the wound in a star burst pattern.

Abbey walked in the front door with bags of groceries. I was so relieved to see him. He saw Bradley in the corner and me on the sofa and immediately spotted the bandages. I told him in a few words what had happened; my fall and Bradley's treatment. Abbey's face turned red; he went ballistic. He immediately yelled at Bradley. "You fucking moron! Don't ever, ever touch Miles. You're a quack. Get lost!" Abbey grabbed the house first aid kit, sterile cotton balls and hydrogen peroxide. He gently pulled off the star of bandages and meticulously cleaned the wound, something Bradley hadn't bothered to do. Abbey intentionally left the wound uncovered to let it air out and form a scab.

Exhausted, Abbey and I retired to our bedroom for a welcome nap. I started calling Abbey, Dr. Abbey. I felt tremendous relief as he held me in his arms. Never again will I entrust my medical care to Bradley. Abbey started a game of doctor patient role-playing. "So Miles, let the doctor examine your butt tan line. It looks very healthy indeed. And what's this large protrusion I see? Yes, I think my patient definitely needs a thorough examination." "Please proceed, Dr. Abbey. The patient is more than ready."

WENDELL

It's a common story amongst us gay men. I played jacks with my sisters, rather than football with my brother. I dreaded P.E. I never played sports in high school or college. Guys like me were called sissies, even by our mothers. I played the piano, not team sports. They called me a wimp, not a hunk. It wasn't until I came out at twenty-three that I dared go inside a gym. Of course, it had to be a gay gym, the Chelsea in New York City; that made it easier, the guys there were just like me, except they had muscles. I figured I'd get some myself. Why not? What was the alternative? I wasn't going to be a sissy my whole life. To my surprise, I soon enough turned into a "regular," after dinner every night for an hour or two. I loved the gym. The guys were friendly, not to mention sexy, dressed in skimpy gym shorts with tank tops. Sure, I can do that. By the time I showed up in the Pines I had a few muscles myself. I was ready for the next step. The Pines was something else. It was my dream gym, as if I died and gone to heaven.

The Pines gym was outdoors, poolside to the Botel. Run by a friendly guy named Jack, a real Adonis. Strictly free weights. All under a huge white tent. I loved it. Being outdoors was so much better than the clammy indoor Chelsea in the city. Plus, you could workout shirtless if you brought your own towel for the bench. I really enjoyed that aspect, looking at all those gorgeous hunks with tons of muscles in tiny gym shorts. Trevor soon became my gym buddy. We were the only ones in the house who took the gym seriously. Unfortunately, Abbey is lukewarm on gyms in general. He just sees the work, not the payback. Not like me. I enjoy the burn afterwards. I can feel my body. I feel alive.

Trevor and I established a routine. We'd be up at sunrise. Before heading off, we'd enjoy a quick bowl of granola together, usually in silence. Trevor and I aren't big on small talk. We just like being together. We'd show up when the place opened at 6:30 for the hard core. I guess we were part of that elite group, the so-called "hard core." We didn't really care about the label. We just loved working out with our gay brothers. They were our family. Jack always welcomed the guys with a warm hug. He was terrific. The first thing Jack would do each morning as he opened the door was to rate the sex he had the night before on a scale of one to ten. "Last night was very nice! A German guy from Berlin. I'd give him a solid 8.5. I always enjoy those German queens!" I noticed it seemed like Jack had more great sex than everybody else put together. No problem, I liked the image in my head of our Jack, a loveable porno star.

Trevor was built solid like a wrestler. Nice and chunky. Great upper body. I envied him. I'm obsessed with six-pack abs. I'm finally starting to show a little something after more than three years of solid workouts daily. It doesn't come easy for me for some reason. I have the wrong body type. I'm an ectomorph, long and lanky. Trevor's a mesomorph, rectangular and boxy. But the guys at the Botel gym don't care; they are all supportive. They spot for me and cheer me on for one more rep, and then another, just when I think I'm finished. They're terrific. What a change from growing up as a sissy in Albuquerque with no muscles. I showed them. We all did. We're in charge now.

Middle of the summer a new guy showed up in a designer's gym outfit. Mr. Full of Himself. What a jerk. He monopolized the equipment, always dropping the free weights from three feet, moaning and grunting like a drama queen. He cut in on Trevor without even asking. Trevor took him on. I was so proud of him. He told him to his face that our gym was not a place for bullies and he wasn't welcome. The guy left and never returned.

I'd have to say the greatest inspiration in the gym came from Wendell. He became my gym hero. Wendell was a partial quadriplegic, the victim of a horrible car accident. Both his legs were paralyzed from the waist down. Thankfully, he could still use his hands and arms. Wendell never felt sorry for himself. After the accident, his boyfriend flipped out and moved out. Wendell hired a personal trainer the next day and went to work on his upper body. He'd spend two to three hours in the gym each day, working out religiously. Wendell always had an extremely handsome face, movie star material, but with his shirt off, and his new muscles sharply defined, he looked like a Roman God. He'd zip around the equipment in his wheelchair working out harder than the rest of us put together. Wendell was a Southern boy, as charming as they came with his thick drawl. "Well, how the hell are you?" He'd gladly spot for me anytime. What an honor. On Wendell's birthday in August, Jack closed early and threw a birthday party for Wendell complete with ample room for dancing on the pool deck. He played plenty of Wendell's favorite music, especially Doris Day. When that dreamy number came up, I asked Wendell for the dance. I held his head from the side kissing his ear, my head on his shoulder, the other hand on his massive bare chest. We were in love. We didn't even notice the wheelchair as Doris sang her all-time hit record *Tammy*.

After a good long workout I'd always enjoy a warm outdoor shower at 124 Sunset, followed by a naked dip in the pool with Trevor and Abbey, my best buddy and my true love. Trevor swam laps while Abbey and I played tag. Trevor always retired to the empty living room to listen to his beloved J.S. Bach, or even better yet, some angelic English boys' choir on his fancy headphones. Trevor soon drifted off to his dear alma mater Cambridge.

After tucking him in, we'd tip toe past and steal away for a long walk along the beach to Cherry Grove or maybe Water Island. Now that was a real schlep. Water Island is a good hour walk from the Pines along the ocean. But it's super beautiful. Completely unspoiled. It's nice and secluded. The perfect place along the way to make love in the dunes. I thanked God for keeping my beautiful Abbey safe. As I thought of Wendell, I kissed Abbey all over his head; I mussed his thick black hair. He didn't care in the least bit. It tickled. I love it when Abbey laughs.

CHRISTO

One late afternoon mid-summer we noticed Bradley was busy spread out on the front deck working intensely on some solo project. He had a pile of white sheets a tall step ladder and a steel tape measure. What the hell was he up to? The front deck is very visible from the boardwalk. We were a little concerned. We knew Ralph was busy in the kitchen making Abbey his vitello tonnato. We were very curious what Bradley was up to. I said I'd handle it since Bradley was always more comfortable around me. We slowly slid open the living room slider and stepped onto the deck.

"Hey, Brad Buddy, what are you up to? Do you need a hand?" "Oh, it's just an art project I'm doing with Ralph. We're doing a Christo number on the house." Oh my God, this could be a disaster, but I stayed calm. "Wow! That sounds exciting. What will it look like?" Bradley explained he's hanging white sheets from the black wood beams that run over the front deck. "Don't worry, the staples will be completely hidden and I'll pull them all out once we take it down. It's just for a few weeks; until the Pines Art Show is over."

As he explained it, I realized he's really dead serious. He's totally into it. He gets me interested as well. Abbey and I are both Christo addicts so we pay attention. He plans to hang a dozen sheets in parallel rows, all running in the same direction, the same direction as the house. They would all hang free above the deck from the overhead beams, moving slowly in the breeze, or completely still when it was calm. The sheets would appear to be sliding left to right or vice versa. It would occupy the deck, but at the same time make it look empty. It will look completely different from the boardwalk and from inside looking out of the living room. It actually sounded rather cool. I made a few detailed suggestions about the installation which he really appreciated. Feeling much more relaxed, I left Bradley to do his thing. He had me hooked.

Bradley's Christo installation was a big hit. It was officially entered into the Pines Art Show and won a second-place ribbon for the best Environmental Art. It was actually very beautiful and it truly enhanced the Japanese feel of the house. Guys would stop dead in their tracks and just stare at the front of the house for minutes. It really calmed people down. Not a bad thing. Quite a change from your typical disco dancing in the Pavilion. I congratulated Bradley. It was the first time the whole house really rallied around him. I could see he was really moved. For the first time, he really felt part of the house. Of course, I gave him a big hug. Ralph was so proud of Bradley. He baked an elaborate white layer cake. It had twelve layers, one layer for each sheet on the deck. Murray threw an open-house neighborhood party with guys dancing on the deck between the sheets. It was cool! Bradley even got to play his favorite Swing Out Sister.

THE INVASION

It was certainly a highpoint of the season. July 4th, Cherry Grove invaded the Pines. It sounded like fun. We'd see. It was pretty wild. The residents of the Grove dressed up in drag, boarded the Fire Island Clipper over to the Pines, which they then invaded without any resistance at all, taking over the harbor to the delight of the waiting Pines men who had turned out shirtless, en masse, to welcome them with hoots and hollers. The least the Pines men could do was to offer our colorful guests free cocktails. This all took place at noon in broad daylight and lasted most of the afternoon.

Abbey got talking to one particularly cute milk maid named Henry. His white scalloped apron over his sky-blue dress was totally innocent, but his chiseled gym bod underneath it was still detectible and extremely sexy. His curly brown hair and boyish smile was right out of *The Sound of Music*. Of course, Henry had the most adorable English accent. It was authentic. Henry was from Liverpool, home of the Beatles. Henry could easily pass as a Beatle himself. He was super cute. Abbey and I offered to give Henry the full tour of our tiny harbor, stopping for a beer in Crews Quarters to introduce Henry to Abbey's favorite bartender Mark and his buddies. They made a fuss over Henry and his milk maid's dress. Henry turned beet red. The poor lad was starving, so we treated him to a Pines legendary meal—our special chicken cutlet sandwich from the Pines Pantry. Pricey, but worth it for Henry.

Abbey asked Henry if he'd like to go for a swim back at our house on Sunset. Henry lit up. "I'm kind of new to this drag thing. I wouldn't mind shedding the dress if you can excuse me swimming in the nude." "I'm sure we'll have no problem with that at all. We'll all go skinny-dipping."

When we walked into the house, Trevor and Donald were in lounge chairs on the pool deck drinking beers. When they heard Henry's English accent they both tuned in and went completely bonkers. At first they wouldn't let Henry take off his dress, but soon agreed to the plan we'd worked out. So we all stripped naked and jumped into the pool. Ralph and Bradley heard the commotion and soon joined in. I'm sure I wasn't the only one to notice that our guest Henry was extremely well endowed. Ralph kept on his black Speedo's so he could demonstrate his diving expertise. Bradley is like me; he swims in the nude all the time.

Donald and Trevor kept their trunks on and stayed in their chairs, completely fixated on the boy. Trevor asked Henry if he'd like a beer. Henry said sure and asked for some chips. Donald mentioned he was also from Liverpool, but played it down. "I'm just your typical English Limey." Henry smiled.

Abbey pulled me aside and told me he thought Henry might be a cock tease. The dress was just an act. He suggested we have a little fun with Henry. "Hey Henry Buddy, seeing that you're our houseguest and we all really like you a lot, how'd you like to relax while we each give you a little head in the privacy of our outdoor shower?" Henry blushed deep red and laughed nervously. His mischievous smile told us he was all in. So we each blew him, taking turns, one guy at a time in the outdoor spiral shower. Henry wasn't as naïve as he looked. He easily played the role of a seasoned street hustler. Of course, it didn't hurt he was half our age, young and hung, horny and insatiable. What a great way to celebrate the Invasion. When we were all done licking our chops, Henry emerged from the shower enclosure with an enormous grin on his face. We gave him a standing ovation complete with hoots and hollers.

Abbey and I walked Henry back to the harbor in his maiden's outfit. We exchanged contact info for the future. The ferry was loading for the return trip to the Grove. Henry excused himself to take a quick leak in the Pavilion men's room. When he reappeared the milk maid's outfit was gone. Henry blushed yet again. He was now wearing white spandex gym shorts and a tight red tank top. He had a serious gym bod. Actually, he appeared to be equally comfortable playing a bold hustler or a shy milk maid. We smiled and waved as Henry boarded the ferry. We stayed on the dock for the official sendoff, blowing a dozen kisses to Henry, who was looking down from the upper deck, one hand waving the maiden's handkerchief, the other squeezing his crotch. The guy was either an adorable milk maid or an insatiable hustler. Take your pick. Still, all things considered, it was a near perfect afternoon in the Pines.

FIRST CALLING

The first phone call came from San Francisco.

It was Philip.
Short and sweet.
He has full blown AIDS.
He called us to say goodbye.
There are no treatment options.
They told Jim he has only six weeks at most.

That is how it works now.
AIDS is a death sentence.
Non-negotiable.
Final.

Abbey and I were best men at Jim and Philip's wedding last summer.
It was a glorious, clear sunny day in Sausalito.

Harken ye angels!
Take my Buddy Philip to heaven.

MARRAKECH REDUX

It was Labor Day weekend. The season was really going by quickly. Abbey and I left work early on Friday to catch the three o'clock ferry to the Pines. Abbey spotted Nick and Jeremy on the upper deck. Nick is our CPA. Jeremy is an architect in the hospitality industry. He was at Syracuse University when I was an hour south at Cornell. We'd debate which town got more snow. I don't miss winters in Upstate New York.

Nick and Jeremy are old friends. We see them at the beach and over the long winter at their second home in Woodstock. They are a couple of hippies, especially Jeremy. He's a vegan, really into alternative medicine, meditation, hands-on healing and pot. He's high half the time. I really like him. He's cool, generous and super sexy. We often sit together on the beach in our beach chairs under umbrellas. Jeremy likes to rate the butts on the guys as they sashay past in their Speedos. He's a bubble butt kind of guy. I guess I am also. Nick and Jeremy recently closed on a studio apartment in the Pines Co-ops. We're jealous. Maybe someday. Abbey and I often walk around the harbor at night looking up into the lit apartments in the Co-ops with their pitched ceilings, their angled roofscape, that always reminds me of a fleet of docked sailboats. Jeremy asks us if we'd like to see the apartment and join them for a simple dinner together. You bet we would! We first stop at the Pantry to pick up some vegan takeout, plus plenty of carrots and celery for munching. Abbey grabs a six-pack of beer, plus one of their vegan apple pies.

The apartment is really quite beautiful with a raised cathedral ceiling and ocean view. Nick passes around a joint and soon we're all feeling nice and mellow, lounging around on pillows on the carpeted floor. Abbey takes off his shirt. "Aren't we all lucky? The Pines is really special." Jeremy asks me if I'd like a massage. "Sounds like just what I really need." He starts with my neck. It's super tight. What hands; they are like a vice. Jeremy has extremely strong hands. I melt slowly. "Miles, let me give you a really deep massage. Abbey has the right idea. Let's all strip naked and have some fun. Are you interested Miles?" "You bet I am Buddy." Nick follows right behind with Abbey. Looks like these guys want an orgy. No surprise really. Something similar happened up in Woodstock when we were snowed in.

Jeremy and Nick spread out several thick beach blankets and pillows on the floor. Clearly, this is a routine they have mastered before. No problem at all. Jeremy grabs the baby oil and a handful of condoms on the coffee table. Abbey and I are facing each other on our stomachs, holding hands, atop piles of pillows. Nick and Jeremy massage our backsides, up and down, head to toe, again and again, especially our soft butts, the tender butt cracks that drive gay guys crazy. They both go nice and slow with plenty of love, working the baby oil in gradually like a couple of pros. I recall those two brown-skinned boy toys we hired in a steamy gay bathhouse in Marrakesh years ago. They were also extremely gentle. Two worlds apart, yet the same. Queer lust, queer desire. It's all so beautiful. Nick and Jeremy took extremely good care of us. They were in no hurry. They took us back to Marrakesh.

REUNION

I learned about Franklin's pool from my friend Kurt. Kurt has that chiseled, blond, German look. Apparently, that's a turn on for Franklin. He's really into it. Guys who fit that description always get special treatment at Franklin's, free lunch, free beers, an invitation into his private tent. Franklin is creative. You never know what he'll propose. I've learned anything is possible with Franklin.

His house is at 491 Bay Walk, the last house on Bay Walk, where it dead-ends at Tarpon. It boasts one of the largest lots in the Pines with bay frontage. The sunsets over the Great South Bay must be spectacular. It's a simple beach house, probably dating back to the first wave of settlers in the fifties. What makes the house so special is the enormous pool with its expansive decks on four sides. Franklin added those. He's an only child. He can't stand to be left alone. That's what makes it into a party house. Franklin is by default, the Party King of the Pines.

Many Pines men will recognize Franklin from his sex shop at the end of Christopher Street in the West Village. It's a gay landmark. We've all been there at one time or another. It really provides an important service to the gay community. Its name, *The Christopher Street Book Store*, is a euphemism. It isn't about books, rather it's about gay men's wildest sex fantasies. Its glass cases are full of erotic sex toys. Its active backroom is world renowned.

Franklin comes to the Pines with his young lover Anthony to get away from the sex shop for a few days at a time. He has created an artificial hidden Garden of Eden that celebrates gay beauty. The noisy, dirty city full of freaks is left behind. In contrast, the Pines is beautiful, full of gorgeous boys lounging around in Speedos in Franklin's pristine pool. There is no trace of AIDS here. Not at the outdoor bar and grill with its free refreshments, nor at the outdoor free-weights gym with its massage station, and most certainly not inside Franklin's golden tent where he enjoys safe sex on cushions with the chosen few. Franklin calls the shots, who's invited in, and who's locked out.

Standing at the locked gate next to Kurt, I feel like I'm cheating, like I'm getting inside by riding on Kurt's coattails. But wait, I have a hidden ace. Three years ago Franklin and I were in the same group therapy. I ask the attendant to give a message to Franklin. "Tell him Miles from Terrence's group therapy is at the gate." I hear the door buzzer. That was sure easy. The attendant asks me to wait, I see Franklin stepping out of his tent with an outstretched hand. He gives me a bear hug. "How are you doing Miles? God, I miss you guys. How's Terrence? You look great Miles. How's Abbey? Let me find Anthony. I know he will want to see you. God, this is really wonderful." I was overwhelmed. I didn't expect to get such a warm welcome from Franklin after three years apart. Suddenly, a flood of memories from our group therapy washes over me. I miss Terrence and my therapy buddies too. I miss Franklin.

A skinny young man with a trim black beard in a long white robe appears before me. It's Anthony. He is calm and radiant. "Welcome Miles. I'm so pleased to see you. I don't get out much. I've thought of you often. I must thank you for all your help, especially all the love you have shown to Franklin and me." "You're most welcome Anthony. You and Franklin were always so easy to love. Please stay safe and may God bless you both. The three of us hugged each other. It was time to part once again. I left Kurt behind. I needed to walk alone for a while. I listened to the mourning doves. I thought of Philip. I already missed him. As I turned onto Sunset, I saw my darling Abbey. He waved and smiled. I started crying. He held me in his arms without saying a word.

GMHC
MORNING PARTY

It was soon becoming the annual gay party to end all gay parties. This year, 1988, would mark the fifth such event. Abbey and I were going with Trevor. Philip had died two weeks prior. We needed a good distraction. Six hundred gay men dancing in swimwear should do nicely. It was a major fundraiser for the Gay Men's Health Crisis (GMHC). It all started a few years back in 1983, as an after-party following an all-night dance party in the Pines Pavilion. The crowd would end up at someone's ocean-front home for more revelry, libations and of course cruising in the daylight which invariably spilled over into the Rack. This year they used the house at 565 Driftwood facing the ocean. There would be music by Michael Jorba with video by Cary Ross. Trevor invited Henry, our milk maid hustler from the Grove. Trevor and Henry were in the middle of an intense love affair. Abbey and I knew it was likely doomed to failure. It was simply too hot to last; but we didn't want to burst Trevor's bubble. Trevor never looked so happy. It turned out Henry had seen Trevor working out in the Chelsea Gym. They had a quickie in the steam room. The day of the Morning Party Trevor and Henry disappeared upstairs searching for an available bedroom.

Abbey and I were both exhausted from dancing all night with all those cute guys in their Speedos. I suggested we check out and head back to the house for a long nap. On the way we spotted John Laub in his sunhat painting the Morning Party from the dunes. It was a large canvas. John didn't see us. Back at Sunset, Ralph was busy in the kitchen. He was planning an elaborate dinner party for ten well-heeled Pines angels to raise money for GMHC. Plus, Murray was going door-to-door to collect thousands of dollars from the neighbors. Guys were feeling generous finally. We've all lost lovers and friends. We felt the need to do something, anything. Beneath all the care-free dancing, we were getting angry. Why were the straights ignoring us? Why don't they care?

We could still hear the live disco music coming from Driftwood. Abbey and I woke up from our long nap. I was aroused from all the overstimulation of the past twelve hours. Thank God, Abbey knows how to handle me. Abbey is truly the best; I'm so lucky. Afterwards, I suggested a walk-thru visit to the Rack, strictly as a couple of curious voyeurs. Abbey was all in. "Sounds like that has my name written all over it."

The Rack was as busy as rush hour in Grand Central Station. GMHC had distributed packets of condoms hanging from the trees, so guys were practicing safe sex. To our complete surprise, we stumbled on Henry from behind, his Speedos down around his ankles, his cute butt on display, his monster dick in an older guy's mouth. No sign of Trevor. Henry didn't notice us. We tiptoed out the back way and headed home. Now what do we tell Trevor? He'll be crushed. We don't have much of a choice. You can't lie to your friends.

When we saw Trevor in the living room we asked him to join us on the back deck. It was empty and quiet. Abbey was about to spill the beans, when Trevor stops him. "I know, I know, I know. You have to understand, I love him completely." Abbey and I were stunned. "Henry and I have been lovers since the shower scene during the Invasion. We clicked instantly. Actually, even before that, we had steam room sex at the Chelsea. Henry has been honest with me from the start; he told me about Marcus. I met Marcus the next day. Marcus is Henry's sugar daddy. He's fifty, more than twice Henry's age. Marcus is a banker. He owns a house in Cherry Grove. He met Henry in the Rack late last season. He adores Henry. He doesn't mind if Henry needs me as well. Threesomes are fine. Whatever. He just doesn't want to lose Henry in his life." What a confession. We were stunned. I quickly realized the man with Henry in the Meat Rack this morning had to be Marcus. Trevor agreed. Henry and Marcus like to have sex out in the open. They're a couple of exhibitionists. Trevor isn't wired that way. He wants Henry all to himself. "Call me old fashioned. I can only love one guy at a time."

It was a remarkable confession. Trevor started crying, Abbey and I hugged him. It was not our place to advise or judge Trevor. As Trevor first put it, "I love him completely." We told Trevor that as long as he truly loved Henry and truly respected Marcus, we would support them both like family. Trevor had chosen a difficult path for himself. We would stand by his side.

The rest of that season, Trevor kept his secret with Abbey and me. He always felt closest to us. The other housemates need not know. Marcus had us over to his place in the Grove for lunch. He was terrific, a beautiful gentle soul. He'd lost his first lover to AIDS at the very beginning of the health crisis. Henry was the replacement. Marcus always practiced safe sex with Henry. Marcus truly loved Henry.

I wanted to help Trevor be more open about his love for Henry. I went ahead and asked Murray and Ralph if they would mind if Henry joined us swimming afternoons at 124. I knew it broke a house rule and they had every right to object. Murray and Ralph were tremendous. It was no problem at all. They really enjoyed Henry's Invasion visit. His brave shower performance earned him a place in their hearts forever. I told Trevor the good news. At first he was nervous, but he calmed down and eventually hugged me. It all turned out for the best. Henry became a regular afternoon visitor. We all swam together nude. Henry bonded with everyone. Trevor's little secret was intact, so all was well at 124 Sunset Walk.

MOTHER'S WEEK

I always crave acceptance. In the Pines that's easy. The Pines is a comfortable illusion. But the real world is another story. Don't count on acceptance there. As a boy I learned that lesson from the playground bully who handed out humiliation. And on Sundays, from the Catholic priest, who told me I was doomed to hell for eternity because I liked boys. Even in college, some hypocrites had the nerve to pity me as the "Pathetic Homo." After coming out, I had to confront the fag bashers hanging outside gay bars, who got their kicks by calling queers like me "Damn Faggot." No, there's not a lot of acceptance in the real world.

Abbey had a great suggestion. "Let's focus on the positives. Let's invite our mothers out to the Pines during the week. They've never met. It's about time. Shirley and Terry. They are both widows with children including gay sons. Two very different women, both strong and independent. It could be fun." The Pines was the perfect setting. It's beautiful and gay love is on full display there. Let them see us as we really are, a loving gay couple, not hidden under layers of crap in the big city. When we mentioned the idea to Murray, he immediately handed us the keys to the house. "It's all yours for the week. No charge. Have a good time with your Moms." That was pure Murray. He's an only child; extremely close to his own mother. He was glad to pitch in. He's a good friend.

We decided it was probably best if Shirley and Terry had the whole house to themselves. That way, they could relax and talk in private. Nick and Jeremy offered their apartment in the Co-ops for us to sleep in. Perfect. Gosh, everybody was being so supportive. They were all cheering us on.

We arranged schedules so the "girls" would meet up at the Sayville Ferry for the crossing to the Pines. It was beautiful weather. As they stepped off the ferry they were both smiling like two excited kids. Good sign. We loaded up our red wagon with their luggage. A cute guy approached us. He was a photographer from *The Advocate*, the world's largest LGBTQ publication. They were doing a story on parents of gay men who summer in the Pines. That's us. What great timing. Wow!

I could see immediately that bringing our two widowed mothers together was bringing Abbey and me closer together too. I hugged him in front of everyone with a passionate kiss. "Excuse me girls, but isn't he just the greatest."

That week we all found unconditional acceptance. It finally felt tangible, completely real. For the first time in my life I felt whole. Terry was my foundation. Abbey was my future. They both bonded. The Pines made all this possible. It's just crazy enough, that anything is possible here.

We got to know each other for the first time. Exactly what we did was not important; it was the doing it together that made the difference. Scrabble on the beach, morning board walks, long lunches, afternoon beach walks, naps, shopping for dinner, cooking, more cooking, sunsets, candlelight dinners, dinners out at the Monster in Cherry Grove, the beach in moonlight, the sound of waves crashing as I drift off to sleep. All sprinkled with conversations, funny stories, laughter and silly jokes. We all had the best of times.

The two ladies had become good friends. We saw them off together from the Pines Harbor. It was better that way, less connected to the real world on the other side. We repeated this pleasant summer ritual for a number of years until Shirley passed away in '94. Terry came once by herself, but it was never the same without Shirley.

We thanked Murray for his annual generosity. We finally arranged a lunch with the girls, together with Murray on the back deck at Sunset. It was shortly after Murray's own mother passed away. I know that simple lunch meant the world to Murray. Friends and family, family and friends. They all belong together.

TIME OUT

It was late September. The Pines was more than just beautiful. She was magnificent, spectacular and deeply moving. The American hollies in the Rack were brilliant red. It felt odd being so totally deserted. Just the ghosts of summer lingering on in the moonlight. We all needed our leather jackets; Trevor, Abbey and I, when we strolled together on the beach at all hours of the day or night. We were all in a funk. We knew we were at a crossroads.

Murray and Ralph were busy lining up shares at 124 Sunset for next season. They were starting to put pressure on Abbey and me to make up our minds. The Darlings had already checked out of Sunset for this season. It doesn't look like they will be coming back. Donald Darling has pressing business in London. He may move back there. Bradley Darling was busy on a second book surveying gay bathhouses across the globe. Abbey pointed out that AIDS might soon spell the end of gay bathhouses as we know them. Bradley Darling acted completely surprised. He has a new boy toy on the side. It looks like he and Donald may soon be history. Abbey and I weren't surprised. We never understood what Donald saw in the kid.

Ralph and Murray are ignoring Trevor as if he's not welcome. Could it be his nonparticipation in the kitchen is wearing them down? Trevor feels he pays his way for everything without question and shouldn't be expected to do more. As the summer wears on, Abbey and I are increasingly becoming house mothers taking care of everyone else. Ralph is pulling back from that role as he and Bradley become more of a couple. Bradley is pressuring Ralph to buy a new apartment with him. It will require both their incomes. Ralph is nervous. His rent-controlled apartment on the Upper West Side is cheap. I can't help but recall Bradley's sarcastic comment from earlier in the season. "What keeps a gay relationship together? Real estate, you dummy."

Abbey thinks we should organize our own smaller house for next season. Save money. We can escape the crazy quack Bradley. We can be in

71

charge for a change. Get people we know who like classical music and quiet time for reading. Guys who can cook. Leave the drama of Sunset behind. Abbey wants to talk to a realtor, see what's out there.

Trevor speaks up. "I never told you guys, I'm sorry, but last season I had a full share with Joe in a quirky beach shack on Neptune owned by a leather couple from Fort Lauderdale. I guess I thought you might hold it against me." My ears perked up. "Are you crazy Trevor? You know I'm a leather queen. Abbey is even more so."

So Trevor told us the whole story. The house sounds perfect. Just two bedrooms with a small space for our guests. Giant kitchen, well equipped. It includes a separate cottage in the back for a single guy. Maybe Ray will join us. I met him through Murray. He's Murray's retired law partner. Ray has full blown AIDS. He's on disability. A really amazing guy. He's an AIDS activist. He's a Texan."

The next morning we have an appointment with the realtor Barry who knows the two old leather queens on Neptune. He starts telling us about parties at the house in the '60s. Barry had fond memories. He takes us over right away. Gunter and Rodney are waiting for us and offer us instant coffee and donuts. Nothing is gourmet. Gunter is a poet; Rodney is his gorgeous Black lover and general handyman. They have been together forever. They must be in their 70s. I liked them both immediately. Abbey did also. They are down to earth, no pretentions. Rodney gave Abbey and me the full tour. It's just the opposite of Sunset, shady and dark, tons of books, antiques, black leather sofas, sex mirrors in the bedrooms, no pool, just a small private deck, dappled sunlight. It looked like the perfect house for relaxation. Of course, I said sign me up. Abbey agreed. Trevor was happy we liked the house. He had fond memories and hoped to repeat them. On the way out he pointed out a stack of vintage COLT magazines on a bookshelf. They were all wrapped in plastic to keep them safe from the salt air. Looks like there will be plenty to keep us all occupied.

SECOND CALLING

The second phone call came from San Francisco.

It was Jim.
He sounded scared.
He has full blown AIDS.
He called us to say goodbye.
Abbey told him to get on AZT.
Jim isn't interested. He just wants to see Philip.

Jim never did pain well.
He was too much of a sissy.
He was a mama's boy,
playing footsie under the table.

Abbey and I were at Jim and Philip's for Christmas,
we drove up the Pacific Coast Highway, to see the towering redwoods.

Harken ye angels!
Take my buddy Jim straight to Philip.

CLOSING HOUSE

Only the home owners are left. All the renters are long gone, back to their tiny apartments in stingy old Manhattan. It's just the few of us and the blessed mourning doves. We have to bundle up for our walks on the ocean. The Sunset fireplace is getting used more than usual. The Pines smells of burning wood. It's quiet, except for the occasional opera aria. The Pavilion is closing on Sunday for the winter. The observant Pines Jews had their ceremony at the ocean's edge last week, Tashlikh. It's where you throw your sins of the last year into the ocean. Abbey passed, he's a reform Jew, they are not so conservative. I like the idea of saying goodbye to your sins. Of course, in Catholicism it's more complicated. Those Catholics really like to get inside your guilt. Confession happens every week amongst the true followers.

We told Murray and Ralph about the house on Neptune. Murray seemed disappointed; Ralph took it too personal. "I thought you all were so happy here." Murray had a good sense of humor. "I always suspected you guys were a bunch of leather queens. Anyway, I'll miss you. You're always welcome to use the pool."

Trevor checked out in early November; he said he couldn't take the cold. I think the real reason was more connected to the deserted Meat Rack. I realized Trevor and I never discussed what we did there. I'd pretend we both did plenty. But I never saw him there. Not even once. Who could say? But ever since Trevor revealed he had spent an entire season on Neptune in "Leather Flats," I was convinced he was a closet leatherman. I figured he must have gone to the Neptune leather parties. My imagination ran wild. I had always found Trevor hot, from our first weekend in the Sunset pool with his red kickboard. I imagined a kinky sex scene with Trevor on the black leather sofa in the Neptune living room. Trevor on top with a leather paddle. Me on the bottom, my butt rosy red.

Murray had a dozen potted Chrysanthemums delivered for the back deck to cheer the place up a bit. He, Ralph and Bradley plan to come out thru Thanksgiving. Ralph will do a turkey. Murray invited Abbey and me, but we're off to my sister's in Providence. But that was a nice gesture. We really connect with Murray. I don't want to lose his friendship.

That's the crazy thing about the Pines. It makes friendships seasonal. All winter we are apart. All summer we are together. It's artificial. I only know Murray in his red Speedos. Rarely in his parka or Georgio Armani suits.

Abbey and I will leave after Halloween next weekend. There is always a Halloween party in the Pavilion for the homeowners. Murray will get Abbey and me in. I'm always a softie when it comes to farewells. I tear up. I'll always cherish my memories of 124 Sunset Walk, the exquisite Japanese house that kept us safe and happy. My new buddies, several friends for life. It was our first season in the Pines, there would be others, some dozen in all. But only one could be the first, full of surprise, mystery and love.

THE FUTURE

Back in the city we already miss the Pines. We think of it all the time. In the gym, those chiseled men who look familiar. At The Saint where the disco music sounds like the latest Pines DJs. And certainly in the baths, where in the orgy room, I'm transported back to the Meat Rack. Abbey suggests a winter get away to the Caribbean, low season. It would be cheap. Maybe Little Dix Bay on British Virgin Gorda. My girlfriend Stephanie raves about it. Murray always recommended it as well. But I'm thinking we may need something more substantial than just another pretty stretch of sandy beach. Maybe that National Historic Trust guided tour of the architecture of Chicago. Gilbert and Sam signed up. It sounds interesting for sure and we love Gilbert and Sam. They have a duplex in the front row of the Co-ops. They like me because I'm an Associate with a world-famous architect. As if that actually means something.

Mid-January we got a call out of the blue from Trevor. He and Henry broke up. Trevor pulled the plug. He couldn't share Henry with Marcus anymore. He really tried to, but it's just not possible. He knows Henry will never leave Marcus. He has to stop fooling himself and let go. Down deep, we knew Trevor was right. He has to move on.

Slowly the memory of the Pines fades. I can't hear the mourning doves when we lie in bed as I rub Abbey's backside. I always love him the most as he falls asleep. Now, all I hear is the traffic on Broadway, nine floors below. The Pines was so civilized, never intrusive, always politely hesitant, like a shy new boyfriend.

Abbey could see I was in a funk. He suggested we call up Trevor for a dinner out together. We could invite Ray so we can all finally meet him. Ray is a foodie. Not only is he a gourmet chef, he frequents Manhattan's four-star restaurants. He loves fish. He recommends we go to Le Bernardin in Midtown. Elegant, tasty and expensive. Ray says it's the kind of restaurant that always gives you a freshly folded napkin on the back of your chair when you get up to use the men's room. I tried it. Ray was on the mark. But what surprised Ray the most that night was the butter stain on his suit jacket. The waiter begged forgiveness and asked him to forward the dry-cleaning bill. Ray didn't hold it against them. The three-hour dinner allowed us to bond. Ray will be most welcome in the house next summer. He has full-blown AIDS, only three T-cells, but he has energy to spare. He chats with Anthony Fauci in Washington DC about AIDS patients' access to the latest drugs. He's a player.

BOMBSHELL

November 1, 1988 is a date I will always remember. That was the day I tested HIV positive. Thankfully, Abbey tested HIV negative. We had put off getting tested for years because there seemed to be no point. We finally went after our first season ended in the Pines. It just felt right given my occasional trips to the Rack. I thought I was always playing safe. Whether there was a direct connection to my new diagnosis was an open question. It seemed likely, but we would never know for certain. There was no point in blaming anyone. I felt a little cheated. But Abbey, my true sweetheart, never blamed me, not even once.

Testing positive back then was a death sentence. There were no treatments available. Zero. I felt numb. My doctor pretty much just walked out of the examination room saying next to nothing. The only good news was my immune system was still intact, fighting the virus. I had a T-cell count of 670. That was in the normal healthy range. That meant I had time. How much time, was an open question. I turned to Abbey; he was pale. I told him, "I will do whatever it takes to stay healthy. I'm not going to die from this thing."

A few weeks later we had a follow-up appointment with the same doctor. He was pessimistic. I was furious with him. I felt he was selling me short. The last straw were his parting words of advice. "Think short-term Miles. You know that Co-op you're thinking of buying? Well, rent it instead." We were offended. Within a week Abbey found me a new AIDS doctor, Alex, who would have a very different attitude. I was on board 100%. Abbey and Alex would be my team. They would keep me alive.

SEASON TWO
1989

A New Beginning

At last, the Memorial Day weekend arrived. Abbey and I were on the afternoon ferry to the Pines. Rodney and Gunter handed over the keys to Leather Flats on Neptune. Ray was already installed in the cottage out back. Trevor would be arriving Saturday morning. Trevor was taking a half share this time around, every other weekend. Tim and Paul would be taking the other half share. That made a total of only four or five housemates, depending on the weekend. Nice and small. That left one tiny bedroom open for guests, although with this group, guests would probably be few and far between. Tim was another AIDS lawyer working with AIDS patients who are being forced out of their apartments. He was an old friend of Ray's. Tim's lover was Paul, a librarian at the main New York Public Library on Fifth Avenue. Ray told us they were a quiet leather couple into kinky sex. Ray said we'd probably not see a lot of them since they are very private. Ray chuckled, "You'll probably hear slaps and moans of pleasure through the walls." That was a good point. We'd encountered this issue before at Sunset. All the walls at Neptune were made of solid wood planks, not your typical sheetrock, so sound went right through the wide-open cracks.

Those wood plank walls were the dominant characteristic of Neptune. They gave it its soul. Over the decades and the hundreds of log fires in the cast iron stove, those planks had turned a deep, dark brown, almost black. The bungalow had a dark, mysterious feel, definitely masculine, definitely sexually charged. That's what drew us all to it. The promise of extraordinary sex.

The enormous kitchen was another story entirely. It was really two kitchens with two sinks and two refrigerators. The walls were painted a bright yellow. The dishes in the cupboards were yellow as well. Gunter had painted yellow sunbursts on the paned windows. This stark contrast with the rest of the house seemed deliberate. The kitchen was the social center. The living room/dining room were for entertaining guests over dinner parties at night.

The bedrooms with their long, low horizontal sex mirrors on each side of the bed were strictly for sex, queer sex, the more, the better.

The house was right in the middle of a mature grove of holly trees. The sun rarely came through the small windows. When the summer heat became unbearable, we covered the flat roof with aluminum foil to reflect the sun's rays. It made a huge difference.

My favorite space in the house was definitely the intimate living room. It was perfect for reading or listening to music on the black leather sofas with their green glass library floor lamps. In the center, it had a small wrought-iron chandelier, which held a dozen votive candles. It was Ray's favorite. He made sure we lit the candles every night. The walls of the living room were lined in bookcases full of books wrapped in plastic to protect them from the salt air. Lots of poetry books belonging to Gunter and plenty of porno belonging to Rodney. Gunter and Rodney loved antiques, blue and white China pieces, brass figurines, oil paintings of nude men, even a couple of *Tom of Finland* drawings. A pair of ceramic turquoise Foo Dogs stood guard over the living room.

That first Saturday night's dinner was very special. Just the four of us. Ray made his perfect greaseless fried chicken. For dessert, Abbey served fresh fruit topped with his homemade whipped cream. Ray insisted on a dash of his favorite Calvados in the whipped cream. That quickly turned into a Neptune house tradition at dinner every night.

What a contrast with dinner at 124 Sunset Walk. Of course, we missed Ralph's cooking, but we didn't miss Bradley's sarcasm. Trevor put J.S. Bach on the stereo. I dimmed the lights. Ray lit the candles. Abbey told us a very dirty joke. We all laughed tears. We were a new family.

Making
New Friends

Our second weekend on Neptune would be with Tim and Paul, who took over Trevor's bedroom when he was away. Abbey and I were really looking forward to meeting them. They are both a little older than us. They just turned forty. Tim was clearly a serious body builder. He was built solid. He was dressed like a leatherman in black 501s, a black leather vest over a tight white Calvin Klein tee. Paul was just the opposite, extremely tall and slinky. He dressed like an androgynous hippie in denim bell bottoms and a tie-dye t-shirt. He looked like Peter Fonda in *Easy Rider*. They both liked the general feel of the house. They fit right in. Tim looked over the free weights on the rear deck. Paul tuned into the books in the living room. "God, these guys are really into vintage porn. This stuff is worth a small fortune." I'm thinking to myself, I really have to thank Ray for bringing Tim and Paul into our lives. I always suspected Ray had a soft spot for leather queens.

While Abbey and I were busy making drinks in the kitchen, Tim and Paul disappeared into their bedroom. I soon detected very heavy breathing from Tim. The bed was making a loud, rhythmic thumping sound. It had to be sex. Paul was moaning, "Fuck your baby." Louder and louder. Total silence. A minute later, to my astonishment, I saw Paul swaying nude at the outdoor shower on the back deck as he crooned to Procol Harum's *A Salty Dog*. He was definitely awash at sea. He must have found the back exit door from their bathroom that goes around the side of the house. I couldn't help but focus on his enormous erection. Tim stepped out of the bedroom into the living room adjusting his thick leather belt as he walked. He had a broad smile on his face. He looked terrific. "We were just trying out the mattress. Glad to report it's perfect! Those sex mirrors are really nice too, I mean really nice, I'm sure we will be happy here."

After that performance, I figured we owed them a thank you. I stripped down and hopped into the outdoor shower. Paul was delighted to see me as I rubbed lavender soap on his backside. I hollered over to Abbey and Tim. "The water is nice and warm. Plenty of room for everyone."

So that's how we met our new friends Tim and Paul. They were super cool. Always up for a little casual sex. They never hung out on the beach. They preferred nude sunbathing on our back deck with friends, sex when it feels right. They insisted Abbey and I join them. Two weeks later, I mentioned this all to our hot tub buddies Stan and George. I figured this was right up their alley. "Sure, absolutely, bring them over on Sunday morning. You still know the address, right? We'll pick up beers and chips and dip. Wear your Speedos." It went so well, I decided to approach Franklin and Anthony on Bay Walk. Well, that was a homerun! Franklin and Tim really hit it off with all those muscles. They retired to the golden tent for half an hour with the drapes closed. Anthony and Paul were a natural fit. Anthony served cookies while giving Paul a full body massage on pillows by the pool. Paul talked him into some pretty kinky sex along the way. Afterwards, Anthony confessed to me, he had a ball.

Of course, Tim and Paul were interested in the Rack. They'd never been and wanted some tips. We said sure, especially under a full moon. We all went together with plenty of condoms. Tim and Paul ended up making love with each other. It was so sweet. They really adore each other. So different, but somehow so right.

Poor Ray was feeling completely left out, so Abbey proposed a little orgy on the back deck. Maybe even spilling into the living room or the bedrooms. Something out of the old days. Like those infamous leather parties on Neptune, that everybody still raves about. Sure, and why not? We invited Ray and Trevor, plus Stan and George as well as Franklin and Anthony. It was an enormous success. I could feel the love. It was fantastic. Men loving men. Nobody dared to even think of AIDS. At least not until the next morning when guilt rose to the surface and everyone looked a little anxious.

TREMORS

Was it just a coincidence? We arrived Friday from the city to discover the giant storage shed on the back deck was leaning over the edge about to split open, spilling Rodney and Gunter's personal crap all over the pristine ground some eight feet below. An old television, boxes of old *Drummer* issues, broken umbrellas, an old vacuum, several leather jackets plus chaps and paddles, half a dozen boxes of VHS porno videos. Even a box of vintage Super 8 open reels. It's all garbage really. Rodney and Gunter are extremely cheap. They save everything.

We called up Barry. Rodney will make a trip up from Fort Lauderdale. He'll drive. It will take a few days. We're nervous the whole shed will be gone by then. Then at dinner the same night, we're all sitting around the table enjoying my chicken enchiladas, when Ray's caned café seat splits wide open, sending Ray's ass to the floor. We're all laughing hysterically, everybody except Ray. The last straw was later that weekend when the floorboards in front of the front door gave way as Abbey was carrying in a couple gallons of bottled water. It was almost a repeat scene of my horrible accident on Sunset last summer with the quack Bradley.

What were the odds of all three of these events happening on the same weekend? It must have been a full moon. Abbey volunteered to do the research on chairs over his lunch hour and then order new dining chairs from the Door Store in the city. He found an amazing deal of six new caned café chairs for a hundred dollars. Rodney said no way. He only budgeted fifty dollars total. When Abbey told Ray what happened, Ray went crazy. He read Barry the riot act. Buy the chairs Abbey picked out or else see him in court. Within a few hours word came down that the deal Abbey found was acceptable after all.

The truth is the house was held together with duct tape and bungee cords. It was all the product of Rodney's ingenuity. But he was no contractor.

It could all come tumbling down at any moment. Imagine what went on in those leather parties with a dozen guys on the rear deck having an orgy. It was crazy. But at night in the candlelight it all looked so wonderful. Just another Pines illusion. It's magic while it lasts.

DANCE CARD

The first summer at Neptune was turning out to be more sociable than I expected. An old boyfriend of Abbey's was staying in a house nearby. Huey was a bit of a prima donna; he was a British choreographer that Abbey met in a West Village leather bar years ago. They had a summer fling. Huey was full of himself. He'd always drop in unannounced in his red Speedos. I got the impression he was looking for Abbey alone for a little action on the side. I resented him. Frankly, I felt he was a bad influence on Abbey. Huey was a borderline alcoholic and a chain smoker. Abbey had stopped smoking to please me. I knew it wasn't at all easy for Abbey to stop. It meant the world to me. Huey was oblivious. Plus, he was secretive. Not once did he show us the ocean-front house he was supposedly staying in. I doubt it was real. But Abbey is so generous, he had Huey over for dinner more than once. Ray confided in me; "He's trouble." As if I didn't know that.

When Trevor was around we arranged a dinner on Neptune for Murray and Ralph. Ray and Murray were old law firm partners. They aren't terribly fond of each other, but they behaved well for the evening. Ray did the cooking; he wanted to impress Murray. But everyone loosened up when Abbey started telling dirty jokes from Cruise Quarters. His friend Doris, the realtor, owns the bar and is always trying to make Abbey laugh. Doris goes way back in the Pines to the early days. She's a good friend of Abbey's parents, Shirley and Edward. Years ago, Doris had Shirley and Ed out to her house on Midway Walk. It's a small world. Abbey wants to invite Doris for dinner at Neptune sometime soon. She's getting frail, but she's super cool, a real trip. Plus, Doris is a huge supporter of GMHC.

For the Invasion I invited my friend Simon out as our first official guest. I knew he'd appreciate the Neptune house. He's really into leather and showed up in full costume. He didn't go to the beach once; he was strictly in the Rack the whole weekend. I made sure he came out during a full moon to get the full experience. He brought a German guy back to the house late Saturday night. They kept Abbey and me awake with their nonstop sex all night long. In the morning at the dining table, we had scrambled eggs and exchanged stories from New York City and Berlin leather bars. Helmut spoke perfect English. He wasn't shy in the least bit. He took a long shower outdoors with Simon. They made a hot butch couple.

Middle of the summer, Trevor was feeling lonely and depressed. He finally met up with a new guy named Jim in the Meat Rack. It was during one of those classic Pines moonlit nights. It was love at first sight. Jim is very sexy, intelligent, sober and kind. Perfect for our boy Trevor. Only one problem. Jim has a sugar-daddyish permanent older boyfriend, also named Jim, that is making things next to impossible. The older Jim also has a daughter. Things are getting complicated. Trevor is conflicted. He hardly brings the young Jim around to the house. He feels he has to be secretive around the older sugar daddy. Abbey insisted Jim and Trevor join us for a casual lunch around the glass table on the back deck. After a beer, everybody loosened up and had a great time. To our surprise, Ray started telling outrageous stories from the old days in the Rack. I never realized that Ray was such a serious leatherman himself in his younger days. It was all pretty wild.

KITCHEN DUTY

I think it's pretty accurate to say. Three things occupy the free time of gay men in the Pines. First, strolling the beach in your Speedos, looking for an afternoon playmate. Second, strolling through the Meat Rack in your work boots, looking for an afternoon orgy. And third, most certainly, shopping all morning in the Pines Pantry and then cooking all afternoon, preparing a sublime dinner for a dozen bitchy queens.

Abbey and I fit primarily into the third category. Not exclusively by any measure, but none the less primarily. Ray was the Head Chef, nicknamed "The General." He prepared the menu and provided the recipes. Abbey and I were his First Lieutenants, responsible for all the shopping and food preparation. Trevor, when available, was Ray's reluctant Second Lieutenant, responsible for washing the endless pots and pans.

Ray was an accomplished chef in his own right. Before contracting AIDS he prepared elaborate meals worthy of the White House. Now he only gave instructions, before and after his long afternoon naps. Nonetheless, the dinners we prepared together at Neptune were extraordinary. Ray's greaseless fried chicken, Abbey's Julia Child boeuf bourguignon, Miles's green chili chicken enchiladas from Santa Fe. Our guests left raving. The plates were always licked clean.

Not everything went smoothly in the kitchen. However, most disasters could be traced back to Trevor. Just like the exploding toaster oven at Sunset, Neptune had seen its share of kitchen drama. Ray was busy making homemade Indian raita for his elaborate Indian dinner. He was draining the yogurt in a cheesecloth sack suspended over the kitchen sink. The process takes several hours as the water slowly drips through the cheesecloth. Trevor strolled through the Neptune kitchen and was drawn inexplicably to the soft moist squishy white sack. He started squeezing it like a lover might squeeze your testicle during sex. More and more pressure. Trevor couldn't stop himself.

He went temporarily nuts, as the sack exploded, spewing yogurt all over the kitchen walls and ceiling.

Trevor felt badly. He was always looking for a way to pitch in. But for Trevor, "the kitchen is a dangerous place."

I was busy sauteing finely chopped onions in olive oil for my favorite pasta sauce. It's an old Roman recipe that uses a cup of red wine. You're supposed to add the wine slowly so the onions have time to absorb it. Well, Trevor sees what I'm up to, and offers to help. I ask him to just pour in a little of the red wine from the measuring cup. Trevor goes crazy, again for no explicable reason. From a distance of over six feet, he grabs the measuring cup full of wine, and literally tosses the liquid contents high into the air in the general direction of the pan. I'm stunned! The airborne wine hits the red-hot oil and explodes all over the stove. I start yelling like a maniac. "Trevor, get out of the kitchen, right now. You are banished from the kitchen for life."

DAVID DE ROTHSCHILD

Shirley and Terry were on board for their second Pines visit in two years. Little did they know what lay ahead. The Neptune house easily passed their casual inspection. They both thought it was very charming. They each had their own bedroom and bathroom. Abbey and I slept over at Nick and Jeremy's studio in the Co-ops. We retired all the homoerotic art to the back of the closet. The horizontal sex mirrors in the bedrooms were tucked under the back deck for the week. We took the valuable pair of Tom of Finland drawings off the wall and delivered them safely to 124 Sunset to hang temporarily in the master bedroom. The girls seemed very comfortable on Neptune. If they noticed anything too peculiar, they kept it to themselves.

They liked the suggestion of dinner out in Cherry Grove. The Monster had a good selection of seafood which appealed to Terry. We decided a walk through the Meat Rack was too fraught with peril. Imagine if we came upon an orgy scene? Oh my God. Instead, we chose the water taxi. They enjoyed the tacky tourist shops in town. The girls were interested in a cocktail before dinner, so we took them to Top of the Bay, an upstairs restaurant and bar overlooking the bay. Abbey excused himself for the men's room. When he returned, Shirley was in the arms of some dizzy queen, disco dancing to *Macho Man,* having the time of her life. Abbey immediately noticed the cheap hair piece, the pint of cologne and the pretentious cigarette holder. Shirley had fallen into a trap. But she was in heaven. It had been years since a man paid her so much attention. When Abbey asked her who he was, she said "Why darling Abbey, this is David de Rothschild. He's invited us all over to his fabulous house nearby for another cocktail." Terry was already out the door with David. His house was pure Grove; a dozen pastel colors with a name posted over the door "Last Call." Oh no. David had his arms around Terry. They were slow dancing in his living room. Terry was all excited. "David, you are a very good dancer. Did anyone ever tell you that you look just like Liberace? You even sound like him." That was the last straw. "Okay girls. Let's round it up. The bus is leaving. We have five o'clock dinner reservations at the Monster." Abbey was busy pushing the girls out the door as I confronted David. "You really ought to be ashamed of yourself. These ladies are widows. We're their sons. Shame on you."

The girls both had a wonderful time, in spite of Abbey and me. They talked about it the whole week. I think they actually enjoyed the Grove more than the Pines. "It's so colorful. And the men are so friendly." They were both impressed with David's glass paperweight collection. That and his superior dancing. We ran into John Laub at the dock for the water taxi back to the Pines. I introduced the girls to John. I told Terry that John was the leading landscape painter practicing in the Pines; he shows his work in a major gallery on 57th Street in Manhattan. She was impressed. We didn't tell them John has full blown AIDS. I told John that Terry was a serious ceramicist. Terry blushed. She's so modest about her artwork.

In the water taxi back to the Pines, Abbey told John all about our run-in with David de Rothschild. John rolled his eyes. "David is a big phony, a total fraud. He isn't a Rothschild. He befriends wealthy widows and then twiddles out their bank account numbers. He's bad news."

CHEST OF TOYS

That first summer on Neptune I got an education. When we checked in with Rodney and Gunter that first weekend on Memorial Day, Rodney discretely pulled me aside into the master bedroom and showed me a locked steel chest sitting on the floor in a corner. He handed me a key. "I want to entrust to you the contents of this chest. Please take good care of it." Rodney asked me to open the top. Inside was a treasure trove of sex toys which Rodney had collected over five decades. I was touched. What an acknowledgment. I thanked him with a hug. I asked him. "But why me?" "I think you know why. These are toys shared by leathermen making love. I've watched you. I think I know you. You will handle these things with love and respect. Am I right?" "Yes Sir, you are right. I give you my word. May I share them with my lover Abbey?" "Of course, but I give you alone the responsibility of caring for these items." We shook hands and hugged. I closed the top and locked the bolt placing the key safe in my front pocket. When Abbey saw me later he asked if I was all right. I told him I was a little shaken up, but that I'd be fine. Abbey kissed me and held me tight. He told me that whatever it was, we would get through it together.

I didn't tell Abbey right away. I wanted to do it in a way that respected Rodney and Gunter and was also an extension of the love making I already shared with Abbey. I knew Abbey would know the way forward. We opened the chest together when we knew no one would be around. It was like Christmas presents for gay men. Sex toys of every description. Many old vintage items we lingered over in awe. We oiled each piece carefully, buffing with clean white cloths. They were really beautiful expressions of gay sex between men. I guess Rodney really knew me well. I was the one to care for these love toys. It would be an honor. We christened each piece, one by one. It was a ritual that lasted all summer. Abbey showed me how each piece worked. It was awesome, it was fun. We never showed our housemates the contents of the chest. It was too special, too private. It was just for Abbey and me. It brought us closer together.

Years later I look back on my sex education with Rodney's chest of toys. I still wonder why he singled me out. It's still a mystery. But whatever the reason, I thank Rodney, the kindest leatherman in the Pines.

Dancing
with Death

Initially, it was Ray's brain child. Why not? Throw an over-the-top leather party at Neptune to raise money for ACT UP, the newly founded grass roots organization, AIDS Coalition To Unleash Power. Send out invitations. Ray and John Laub jointly would be the official party co-hosts. It was to take place on Saturday June 21st at our house 388 Neptune Walk starting at ten o'clock to sunrise. Tickets a hundred dollars in advance, two hundred at the door. Everyone will be dying to get in. John's lover Bruce got his sexy buddy George Michael to commit to making an appearance singing dressed in his leather.

It could raise a fortune.

The 1989 AIDS Leather Party would be the first such event in the Pines. We all would pitch in, but it was really John and Ray's baby. They both knew everybody in the Pines gay community. Ray made a hundred phone calls. We never saw Ray so alive. He was really excited.

Ray had the vision. It would be a party unlike any other in the Pines. Dancing yes, unprotected sex no. Condoms yes, fisting no. No hard booze or drugs. Just spring water, beer or punch. Only denim, tie dye, leather or jock straps. No spandex, rubber or polyester. Besides George Michael, the music would include J.S. Bach, Dusty Springfield, Wagner, Laura Nyro, the Mamas and the Papas, the Moody Blues and the Rolling Stones. All AIDS patients will get in free. Doctors on site as needed. No ghosts. Only positive energy, no downers.

As the date of the party was closing in rapidly, Abbey and I volunteered to decorate the house. We decided to use the vintage leather porn that Rodney and Gunter left behind. We carefully tacked it to the wood plank walls so everyone could enjoy it. The greatest hit was Abbey's idea to change all the white light bulbs for red ones that really flatter your skin. Plus, we added black lights that make anything white glow in the dark. Imagine what an old jock strap looked like. We set up a small stage on the back deck for George Michael to sing from, complete with a spot light to lite his cute baby face. We even put dry ice in buckets of water to create heavenly clouds flowing across the floors. It was magic.

The night of the party a line started forming outside our front door at eight-thirty. It must have been at least a hundred guys long, running down Fire Island Boulevard to the Pines Harbor. I never saw so much leather together in one place. Guys dressed in fantastic leather costumes with leather motorcycle caps, leather chaps and leather gloves. Several guys in wheelchairs were being ushered to the front of the line. A couple of guys were riding their Harley's with the engines muted. At ten o'clock sharp Ray opened the doors. He was wearing the most beautiful smile. His eyes were tearing up. "Welcome, my brothers. My home is yours. Play safe." A boisterous cheer went up from the men. I could hear the wailing voice of Dusty Springfield as she belted out her smash hit, "You Don't Have to Say You Love Me."

I started crying as I thought of my best buddy Bob, who by now was surely completely blind. I was such a coward. I was afraid to visit him in Saint Vincent's hospice care. He was probably there alone, waiting for AIDS to hand him over to Death.

I looked around the crowded living room. Abbey gave me a gentle squeeze from behind. Ray blew a kiss to me across the dining table. "Cheer up Miles. We are all in this mess together. Thank you for being here."

GUESTS

It was pretty late in the season. Abbey asked me if we should invite Jerry and Pablo to the house next weekend as our last guests. They can use the tiny guestroom. Sounds great! Absolutely! It will be Tim and Paul's weekend. Trevor will be in California visiting his sister. Pablo and Paul are good friends from their days together at Gay Activists Alliance (GAA). Jerry is Abbey's old therapist going way back. When Abbey finally quit therapy with Jerry six years ago, Jerry and Abbey became close buddies. Actually, Jerry had to throw Abbey out of his group therapy sessions because Abbey was becoming way too comfortable. Abbey could have stayed in therapy forever. He loved it. A lot of guys are that way. They become therapy addicts. I can relate to that. I'm still in therapy with Terrence who I met shortly before Abbey came into my life five years ago. I love both Abbey and Terrence. I think of them both as my co-therapists.

Jerry and Pablo showed up early Friday afternoon with Tim and Paul. Jerry brought special buffalo mozzarella from Balducci's for Ray, plus a fabulous homemade peach pie. They had already gone shopping with Paul in the Pantry for tonight's dinner. Now they were all on the beach, finally relaxing under two rainbow beach umbrellas. Abbey and I joined them in our new Speedos. Pablo gave me a warm hug and a firm slap on the butt. Pablo likes to fool around with me. We dated for a few months before Jerry was in the picture. I guess Pablo never got over me completely.

Jerry is a southern boy from Georgia with the cutest southern accent. That's where he learned to bake pies. He enters them in the state fair and always walks away with a few ribbons. For dinner Jerry dressed in a white tee with a colorful chiffon skirt right out of the Nutcracker. Jerry loves drag and knows how to have fun. He and Abbey had us all laughing tears. Ray brought out the extra special Calvados for Abbey's whipped cream on top of Jerry's peach pie.

Afterwards we all went dancing at the Pavilion. Even Ray joined us. Pablo pulled me off the dance floor and suggested we take a walk on the beach. I told him that was a bad idea. "I don't want to hurt Abbey." Instead, we talked on the steps outside the Pavilion. Pablo still loves me. Abbey understands all this and knows Pablo can't help himself. It's harmless. Pablo is actually a very sensitive guy. He apologized and told me he really admires Abbey and me. He thinks we are a positive role model. Back inside the Pavilion, Abbey was waiting for me. He gave me a warm hug. He is so wonderful. First thing Abbey asks, "How is my sweetheart?" "Thank you for giving me the space. I love you. You know Pablo still has a thing for me. He's so sweet. But he's getting over me slowly. Jerry is great for him."

On the train back to the city we reflected on the weekend. What a homerun. Everyone had such a good time. Jerry and Pablo were perfect guests. They were constantly helping out with the chores. We never saw so much of Tim and Paul. Usually they are so private. Paul and Pedro are obviously very close. Jerry had us laughing tears. And they really bonded with Ray. That was super-nice. Ray can be a challenge.

Abbey leaned over and whispered. "Did it ever occur to you that Jerry and Pablo would be the perfect housemates to replace Trevor for next year?" "Yes, I did. It's so obvious. What a contrast. Yes, but he'll be crushed." "You're right. But it's something to consider. How long can we play babysitters?"

BETRAYAL

Oh, what fools we are, to be blind to love when she finally befriends us. Abbey and I were both wrecks. We had made up our minds. Trevor's departure seemed inevitable, although it wasn't. But that didn't make it any easier. We consulted with Ray. He wasn't surprised. He reluctantly agreed. Ray really likes Trevor, but understands why we are pushing him out. Trevor rarely contributes anything to the house. Ray summed up our wretched situation. "He just doesn't know how to help. He's like a little boy."

So what do you do with a little boy who misbehaves? Give him a spanking, right? Except Trevor would probably like that. He was driving me crazy. We decided to tell him late afternoon on Sunday. Trevor often gave us a ride home. We'd stop on Long Island for a fish supper together along the way. A welcome chance to compare notes from the weekend. Now we'd have to make up some phony excuse. Miles's niece was getting married in New Jersey. Or, Abbey has to attend another AIDS memorial at Saint Mark's Church. I've always been a terrible liar. Nobody ever believes me. Which is usually a good thing. I mean, I hate lying. This is so difficult. I suggest to Abbey that we take an ocean walk to Water Island. That will eat up the time. He agrees. My plan backfires. We just talk nonstop about Trevor, and how he's driving us crazy. Why it's all his fault. How we've never acted this way before, that we're really sorry, but it just isn't working out. We exhausted ourselves just talking around it in circles.

We sat down in the dunes. I started crying. Abbey held me for a long time. I slowly composed myself. I focused on the sound of the ocean, the regular rhythm of the waves. It was very soothing. My head was numb. I didn't have a care in the world. I started talking nonsense, gibberish. Abbey started tickling me. He was driving me crazy. We started rolling around in the warm sand. Abbey was on top of me holding me down against the sand.

It felt good. I surrendered. I welcomed Abbey's total domination over me. I was exhausted.

Strangely, I felt much better. The rough play cleared my head. We walked back to the Pines in silence holding hands. I kissed Abbey on the head, on his soft warm ears that I love so much. We left the ocean and took the stair over the dunes to the start of the boardwalk along Fire Island Boulevard. The sun was mercilessly hot. There was no shade. It's not the pretty side of the Pines; this is the ugly side, the underbelly of the Pines, with its intrusive telephone poles and its ever-present utility trucks. This is the Pines you only see if you are in a hurry to catch the ferry, there are no pretty flower boxes, no guys in Speedos lounging around their pool decks working on their tan lines.

In the distance, I made out the silhouette of Trevor walking slowly towards us. He looked so small and vulnerable. I felt tremendous regret. I recognized Trevor's signature shuffle, the one that always cheered me up. He was carrying his gym bag, the one he always carried to the Botel Gym with me each morning. I started tearing up again. I stopped for a moment. I told myself I'm not going to cry this time. I will be stronger. Trevor deserves that. As he got closer, Trevor waved. I was relieved. Perhaps it's not too late to make things right. He smiles nervously. We waved back. He looks terribly upset. I know that look. It's too late. He stops altogether, leaning forward at the waist. Is he having trouble breathing? I'm concerned he's having a heart attack. But he isn't; I'm overreacting. Finally, he is standing directly in front of us. Trevor speaks. He sounds upset, perhaps even angry, but he keeps his cool and speaks softly and clearly.

"I just spoke to Ray. He told me everything. I'm leaving now." Then a dam broke open. Trevor started crying softly, then he covered his eyes, as if he was embarrassed. Abbey and I felt awful. There was nothing left to do, but accompany Trevor to the ferry dock nearby in total silence. Before stepping on board, Trevor composed himself with tremendous pride, then turned to face each of us, one at a time, speaking perfectly.

"Forgive me, I love you." The ferry whistle announced the boat's imminent departure. I saw Trevor's head and body disappear as he slowly ascended the metal staircase to the upper deck. That was the last time we saw Trevor in Fire Island Pines.

MOVING ON

Rodney and Gunter would be coming up from Fort Lauderdale to close up the Neptune house and sign our new lease for next year. Only Abbey and I went out Friday after work. Ray had a doctor's appointment. We already had a sendoff cake last weekend for Tim and Paul. I really enjoyed their company, especially the hippie librarian Paul. And Tim, the body builder, was also nice to look at wandering around the house in just his yellow BIKE jock strap. He's something.

Barry, the realtor, called to say Rodney and Gunter would check in Saturday morning. They invited us to stay out Saturday night, if we were interested. We could use the second bedroom. Rodney might need a hand from a couple of younger guys in closing up the house. We said sure, it would be an opportunity to get to know Rodney and Gunter a little better. Plus, they had heard on the grapevine that the ACT UP party was the event of the Pines season. Next time they wanted to be invited. We apologized and said next year we'll make sure they are included.

The doorbell rang at ten the next morning. Rodney and Gunter were decked out in their leather jackets. Rodney wears red sweat pants. I mean like all the time. Old timers told us he never wears underwear. His big black boner is always visible running down a leg. I tried not to stare, but soon enough I figured why not? Rodney's proud of God's gift, so why not acknowledge it and show him some respect. As they stepped inside I decided to go for it. "Welcome home guys. Rodney, you look like you're glad to see me." Rodney picked up on my joke immediately. "All in good time, my boy, all things in good time."

After installing the storm windows and consuming Gunter's simple lunch of sandwiches on the back deck, we were all good and happy. Rodney asked if we had tried out the sex toys in his steel chest in the master bedroom. Abbey and I blushed. Abbey spoke up. "We sure did. Thanks a lot. We sort of kept them to ourselves, our little secret. We tried them all out, one at a time. They are really beautiful. We oiled them carefully and buffed them with soft cloths. Thanks a lot." Rodney was touched. He stood up and hugged us. "I knew I could trust you boys, I felt it when I first met you. Let's relax tonight, put a log in the fireplace, open up the chest and have a little fun." I worked extra hard that afternoon, working up a good sweat. I was hot to take up Rodney's invitation. We couldn't wait for darkness to arrive. Of course, Rodney would be the master. He would call the shots. He knew best. He was gentle and thoughtful, always taking super good care of everyone. That last night of the season at Neptune was one for the record books. Rodney was spectacular.

Early Sunday morning we used the back deck outdoor shower one last time. Gunter made his special scrambled eggs with blue cheese. They walked us to the ferry landing. We hugged. We said goodbye until next season, Memorial Day, just around the corner. We shed a tear. Gunter promised to write regularly. Afterall, he is a published poet. As the ferry pulled away from the dock, they waved from the open upper deck. I finally realized then, these two old tired leather queens were our missing fathers, the fathers we never knew. I was proud to have met them, to have shared in their unfiltered love.

SEASON THREE
1990

WINTER

Winters in New York City can be frigid. Especially when the wind blows down those stone and glass canyons. That's when we stay huddled up inside our Manhattan apartments, reminiscing about our summer in the Pines. In Fire Island Pines our social calendars were always full with dinner parties, fundraisers, disco dancing, and cruising in the Rack. In winter we turned into monks, locked inside our cells. Monastic life was boring. We missed the Pines gossip, the thrill of new love, the cute butt on a new guy in his Speedos. Winters in New York City were a bore.

Abbey and I had a few diversions. Like our brothers, we found they mostly revolved around opportunities for casual sex. Trips to the baths, the backrooms, the queer bookstore, the Ramble. Old habits hard to break. But we had one outing that we always looked forward to. That was a visit to Ray's apartment in the Village. Now that was special, never boring. An afternoon visit with Ray was the best. That was like an escape to the Pines.

Ray lived in one of those twelve-story white glazed-brick Greenwich Village Co-ops. They come with gay doormen who hold the door open for you, who keep your Christmas packages and dry-cleaning safe. We always thought they were so civilized. We envied Ray. He lived on an upper floor, but his view was crap compared to ours. We looked at the Empire State Building; Ray faced a light well. Ray lived alone. His German ex-lover Hans had moved out when Ray came down with full-blown AIDS. Ray pointed out this creep Hans in the Pines. He had taken up with a new healthy lover who owned a Horace Gifford house near the ocean. Hans never visited Ray on Neptune. I had always wanted to see the inside of the Gifford house, but now that wasn't likely.

When Ray opened his apartment door in the city, I was never sure if he was glad to see us or not; he had a poker face. That was Ray, always serious. Well, after all, Ray was a major AIDS activist who got return phone calls from

Anthony Fauci in Washington DC. He was an important player. Important people don't smile just because you're waiting for them outside their door.

A visit to Ray's always started with food. Ray's mother in Corpus Christi sent him frozen tamales from Texas by FedEx on dry-ice. They were prepared by a friend of Ray's mom from her temple. Ray was Texas-bred through and through, born in Corpus Christi, one of the few Jewish families in town. In his prime Ray was a serious cook. Those days were in the past. Ray's brilliance in the kitchen was reduced to hot tamales in the microwave. But still, they were delicious.

Ray proudly showed us his Persian rug collection which inspired us to start our own. He had amassed a good dozen Oriental rugs, several beauties. The odd thing was, Ray only collected tiny rugs, the size of doormats, he never bought the large ones you use in a living room. He could easily afford one. That was Ray, always holding back a smile.

Ray mentioned he'd seen Trevor at the Quad Cinema with his new cute boyfriend named Gary. He has a speech impediment of some sort, as if that would matter at all. They just got back from a mini-vacation in Hawaii. Gary is into anything mid-century modern. The kid must be half Trevor's age, adorable, into cats. That's Trevor. "Did he ask about me?" "Nope, not a single word. He seems angry. He blames you for the breakup. He thinks you are a control queen." "Well, he's right about that. Tell him to call us sometime. We really miss him."

THIRD CALLING

The third phone call came very late from Chicago.

It was Dave.
He sounded pissed.
Bob passed away on Sunday.
Dave is staying at Bob's Lake Shore Drive apartment.
The funeral will occur on Wednesday, but only if the sun is shining.
Bob insisted on Handel's *Water Music* in Oak Park Cemetery.

I will definitely be there for Bob.
AIDS will not be Bob's final chapter.
We will witness Bob's ascension into heaven.
I will bring Bob a dozen pure-white lilies.

Abbey and I were at Bob and Dave's Halloween costume party.
Bob was Eliza Doolittle, at the racetrack, in that black and white hat.

Harken Saint Michael the Archangel!
Restore Bob's vision completely. Lift my Buddy Bob into heaven.

THE SWAMP

The landscape painter John Laub was hosting the 1990 Pines Art Show. It won't be in one of those grand Gifford houses, which is normally the case. John and his lover Bruce aren't loaded. This season they are renting a modest house on Bay Walk. That's all right. John knows everybody, so there's bound to be a good turnout for the Art Show. Most of the paintings for sale were John's anyway. He's been unusually busy this past year. He has started painting huge landscapes inspired by Claude Monet. John and Bruce made a pilgrimage to Giverny, France in the spring to see the work of the grandmaster. John's giant new paintings barely fit inside John's living room. It didn't matter. He sold out by the end of the first day.

Abbey spotted a tiny horizontal screen-print in the hallway. It had a Japanese feel. I realized we'd seen the same print in our master bedroom at 124 Sunset. It belonged to Murray. It dated back to Murray's summer fling with John over two years ago. Abbey grabbed the print from the hallway and thanked John. It marked the first Laub in our collection. Over the years three others would follow.

The screen-print measures fourteen inches wide and four inches high. It's a Pines landscape with the edge of a boardwalk in the lower right corner seen at an angle. Higher up in the middle right side is a second boardwalk splaying away at a higher angle. Thick vegetation covers the whole scene with bamboo shoots and flowering rhododendron bushes. What makes this impressionistic painting extraordinary is the choice of colors. John, like his hero Claude Monet, is a brilliant colorist. Almost all of the painting is covered with shades of light and dark green vegetation. The two broken segments of boardwalk provide the only contrast. And what contrast indeed! The lower boardwalk in the corner is a hot pink. The upper boardwalk in the middle is a bright orange. In the lower left, a cobalt blue sky is reflected off swampy water. Indeed, you soon realize, that both boardwalks are built over a swamp. John explained the pink one is Fire Island Boulevard; the other is the walkway to a private house. And therein lies a funny story often repeated in the Pines.

The walk to the hidden house belongs to a successful decorator named Gerard. He's an old friend. After Gerard bought the house, he noticed a thick layer of green moss covering the top of the swamp. It looked like a beautifully trimmed flat lawn. Gerard's house was the last house in the Pines before you get to the Rack. The proximity to the Rack was a major selling feature when Gerard was house shopping. The boardwalk that splits off to Gerard's house looks like a shortcut to the Rack. Gerard would occasionally hear guys in a hurry taking the shortcut. They'd always curse loudly as they fell into the swamp.

Gerard is a clever guy. He noticed the routine of falling into the swamp was especially common during a full moon. The moss turned a silvery gray that looked just like smooth sand. All night long guys were falling into Gerard's giant spider trap. He'd be patiently waiting inside his living room with the screen door open, a clean white bath towel in one hand. After the splash and curse passed, Gerard was off to inspect his catch. If he liked what he saw, he'd hand the poor guy a fresh towel. "Would you like to come inside for a hot shower, while I toss those wet clothes in the washer? It should only take an hour or two. It would give me a chance to get acquainted with Mr. Big Boy."

LEATHER FLATS

Second season at Neptune started off a little strange. The absence of Trevor was felt everywhere. I lost my gym buddy. J.S. Bach on the afternoon stereo always brought Trevor back, lounging on the black leather sofa. Even in the kitchen, Ray's stack of dirty pots and pans made me think of him. Damn you Trevor. Why were you so helpless? Trevor's replacements, Jerry and Pablo, were terrific, but hardly Trevor. Trevor was irreplaceable.

But life went on. Soon our old favorite pastimes returned. Like those wood plank walls that still let the sound pass through them. They provided endless material to feed my hungry imagination. Abbey and I soon knew all about Jerry and Pablo's most private sex lives. Pablo was definitely the top into leather paddles and hand slaps; Jerry was always the bottom, clearly eager to be fucked. Pablo knew just how to please him. As the season wore on, I noticed their wardrobes shifted gradually from Ralph Lauren to Tom of Finland. The house brings out the leather in everyone. It's that mid-day darkness, the walls of books wrapped in plastic just like condoms, the endless porno hidden away in locked bedroom drawers. The house simply reeked of queer sex.

No one missed Trevor in the kitchen. Jerry's southern fried chicken and his homemade pies were simply TDF. The only problem was they equaled or even surpassed Ray's. "The General" was jealous and it showed. Jerry, the therapist, knew just how to handle Ray. Plus, Jerry's gift of a little buffalo mozzarella from Balducci's didn't hurt at all. It's Ray's favorite.

We started to personalize the house, particularly the living room and back deck. Pablo tacked his favorite porno to the wood plank walls using ready-made mat frames. He also installed Rodney's sex sling outback from a tree branch. That always got the most attention from our dinner guests. We had fun. Ray brought out his stuffed armadillo, a childhood prize from Texas. It was good and ugly. Ray installed the beast overhead in the wrought-iron chandelier. I brought out my set of Legos and constructed a six-foot tall art deco skyscraper in the living room on the coffee table. Abbey, the non-observant Jew that he is, installed blue Christmas lights on the rear deck.

Jerry supplied fresh cut flowers for the dining table. When Jerry cooked dinner in the kitchen, he always dressed gay cowboy style in Rodney's black leather chaps, which he'd retrieved from the back shed.

Abbey and I discovered a stash of hidden porn, tucked away in the master bedroom. It was in hidden drawers under the mattress. It was Rodney and Gunter's really good stuff. It had been well used. The pages were stiff from dried cum. We also perfected the placement of Rodney's horizontal sex mirrors, one on each side of the bed. We had perfect close-up views. We fell into a routine of languid sex in the afternoons, when the house was usually empty. Afterwards, we'd take nice long naps or swim in the ocean.

I did some serious reading for a change that summer. Larry Kramer's *Faggots* and Anthony Blunt's monogram *Borromini*. At work, I'm leading the design of a new elementary school on Roosevelt Island. Borromini is an inspiration. Kramer and Blunt make an interesting pair. Both were brilliant. Both were queer. They saw the world through a queer lens, just like I do.

AN
UNSETTLED VISIT

Abbey and I checked in with everyone before inviting Murray and Ralph to dinner Saturday night. Ray was a little nervous, but quickly agreed. Jerry and Pablo don't know them from Adam, so sure, it sounded like fun. Jerry immediately volunteered to bake his peach pie. "The General" Ray will make his fried chicken; I'll make the salad and Abbey will do the grocery and wine shopping. Pablo volunteered to vacuum the house, sweep the deck and set the table for seven.

Ralph arrived with a huge potted rhododendron with red blossoms, which Abbey and I placed prominently on the rear deck. Murray brought two bottles of Dom Perignon Champagne. He gave Ray a warm hug, which I took as a good sign. "You look great Murray. Are you in love?" "Oh, do I wish." Looks like they are both mellowing out at last. We all toasted to friendship and family. We decided beforehand that the music would alternate classical with disco, so everybody got in a little dancing before dinner.

Ralph pulled me into the kitchen and whispered. "Looks like Bradley and I are breaking up. He wants me to buy a new apartment near Lincoln Center with him. It will require both our incomes. I'm nervous. My rent-controlled apartment on the Upper West Side is just fine and it's cheap." I can't help but recall Bradley's sarcastic comment from earlier in the season. "What keeps a gay relationship together? Real estate, you dummy."

After Ray's fried chicken and Jerry's peach pie, Murray admired the books in the bookcases and the erotic antiques. "You guys really have a lot of interesting pieces of art here, don't you? Love that bronze of guys having sex." No one said a word about Pablo's matted vintage porn, but it certainly got plenty of long looks.

I stepped out on the back deck with Murray and Pablo for some fresh air. The sun had already set. The cool night air felt good. Murray took off his shirt. He was sweaty after all that dancing. "You're lucky, you have total privacy here." Murray noticed the sex sling hanging from the giant holly and started laughing nervously. "Oh my God, what's that?" Pablo chuckled. "A sex sling, dummy. Haven't you ever tried one?" "Well, not exactly. I saw one once in action in the Eagle. I admit it looked kinda cool." "Yea, they are way cool all right. Hop in, I'll give you a ride." Pablo also removed his shirt. "Not so fast Pablo. I'll take a rain check."

It was already autumn, late October, another season in the Pines was already winding down. Another Day of Reckoning, an accounting for our actions of the past season. Can my betrayal of Trevor be forgiven? Were my midnight trips to the Meat Rack true or false? Had Abbey and I fulfilled our promise we made to Trevor on the beach that afternoon when we first met two years ago? "Let each of us pledge to look after each other with selfless love. Together we are stronger."

The dinner party left me agitated. The news of Ralph and Bradley's breakup was unsettling. Pablo's display of porno on the walls seemed a little too vulgar. Plus Pablo's casual offer of sling sex with Murray came across as a touch too forward. It all left me super-horny. I told Abbey I was headed to the Rack to let off some steam. He was too tired and told me to play safe. I gave him a warm hug.

The Rack was pitch black tonight, dead quiet, just a sliver of a moon. That suited my solemn mood. All I could make out in the dark was the red tip of his cigar. The fragrant tobacco aroma had me quickly aroused. He removed the cigar from his mouth to replace it with my hard-on. He was starving for cock. His mouth was warm and wet. I slipped on a condom. The sex in the dark was rough and hurried. It was what I craved. I must have cum a record. When we were at last finished, the red tip of his still-lit cigar returned to his sated mouth. He took a long drag on it. I took in the sweet fragrance one more time. Eventually he sighed. "You have one beautiful cock."

NEW DIRECTION

John Laub invited Abbey and me to stop by their apartment in the Co-ops to see a new oil painting. He and Bruce are renting the duplex just for the end of the season. When we showed up, John had the large new canvas hanging over the bed. It was a gorgeous nightscape of the Pines Harbor. Unfortunately, it wasn't for sale. John had already promised it to his brother. John said he was planning on making a couple of screen-prints of the same composition, if we were interested. Absolutely, it would be well worth the wait.

Then we tuned into the apartment. It was also stunning. A minimalist renovation, right up our alley. High cathedral ceilings, lots of glass, a private deck, new kitchen and bath, two bedrooms and a stunning floating staircase with built in sofa that recalled Paul Rudolph at his best. "Wow, what a great apartment." "You should speak to the owner Mandy. He never uses it. He lives in Philadelphia. He's a bit of a nut job, but he might sell it to you if you're interested. The real estate agent is Candy in town. We're checking out in a week. We'll miss the place. It's been nice and quiet."

That's how it all started. It just fell into our laps. But once we spent some time inside, we were hooked. We'd have to back out of the lease at Neptune. But that should be easy with its reputation. Jerry and Pablo weren't renewing and Ray could always take the back bedroom at 124 Sunset. Jerry and Murray have bonded ever since the dinner party and the unresolved sling episode. "Pablo is a big puppy dog. He'll leave you alone. He just wants to have a little fun."

On the way down the Co-op's red spiral stair we ran into a tanned elderly gentleman who was especially friendly. He was wearing jade green boxer swim trunks. He was in great shape for his age, I'd guess he might be ninety. His pectoral muscles were taut and trim. He must have been a swimmer in his prime. "Hello boys. I'm Dell. If you need any help moving in, I have very strong hands. I also give a firm neck massage. But that may cost you. It depends how things go." He made me laugh. I liked him immediately.

He reminded me of my favorite grandfather. Later on, John filled us in. Dell was a retired "garmento" who sold lady's dresses out of his trunk during the Great Depression. He's a Pines legend. He knows everyone. As I passed him, he gave me a distinct pat on the butt. That and a beautiful smile. We could become friends.

On the afternoon train back to the city, we talked of nothing else but the duplex apartment and Dell. Our path was clear. We would buy the apartment, make the owner an offer he can't refuse. But we'll be smart about it. First, sign a rental lease for next season, but include a first option to buy at an agreed upon price. That will get his attention. Since we know he never uses it, the offer should be accepted. The only problem was the owner Mandy was certifiably crazy. We soon found out he didn't just leave the Pines on his own. The Co-op Board actually banned him from occupying the unit, due to his generally bad behavior. Sounds like we'll need some legal help. We decided to consult with Murray. Afterall, Murray is the Pines' leading real estate attorney. He'll know what to do.

HARRY

It's a good thing the realtor Candy was involved. She used to be a third-grade public schoolteacher in Sayville. She was a dyke who knew how to handle playground bullies and weak sissies. She knew Mandy from years back. She also knew of his history as a leading nut job in the Pines. When Mandy refused to hire an attorney to draw up the rental contract and option to buy, Candy approached Mac, the owner of the Pines Liquor Store. Mac was a licensed real estate attorney on the side and offered to draw up papers for Mandy free of charge. Murray even pitched in. Mac, like everyone else in the Pines, just wanted to see Mandy go. He was bad news. Plus, everybody was lining up behind Abbey and me. In just two years' time, we had become close friends with many of the local players. They wanted to welcome Abbey and me as Pines property owners. We were touched. We felt the Pines was our home.

It was all falling into place. When Memorial Day rolled around, Candy called to tell us to get our butts out to the Pines ASAP. Our duplex rental was finally ready for inspection. We were thrilled. Dell met our ferry and invited us to our first meal in the Co-ops. Dell introduced us to our new downstairs neighbors Dave and Richard, both insurance bankers, and our upstairs' neighbor Wolf, a retired eye surgeon.

We kept making mental comparisons to the houses on Sunset and Neptune. Those were both like gay camp for teenagers. The Co-ops were more X-rated for adults and lovers. We fit in better here. Cruising on the grounds was common. Guys hung out in the nude on their decks. Dell wandered up the spiral stair and asked us if we needed anything. When I asked him for his famous neck massage, he gladly stepped inside and gave me a neck massage and then some. He's a very sexy guy and he knows it. The three of us got a little carried away. Now that the ice was broken, we could all relax and get to really know each other better.

Dell filled us in on the backstory of Mandy and his boyfriend Harry, the guy who actually owned the duplex apartment originally. Harry was the Chief Designer at Knoll International. Mandy was his boy toy from the streets of Chicago. When Harry died suddenly from a heart attack at age forty-two, Mandy showed up with a phony will that gave Mandy everything: the Pines duplex, a townhouse in Philadelphia, a ranch outside Santa Fe. Mandy took it all, leaving nothing for Harry's widowed mom.

Dell was Harry's faithful lover for over twenty years. He ended up with nothing as well. Dell has a few pieces of Japanese pottery that Harry gave him before the heart attack. They are by the famous American potter Toshiko Takaezu. Dell showed us the enormous round closed forms. They were extremely beautiful, moon pots with atmospheric glazes. Dell removed them from Harry's apartment before Mandy showed up. Otherwise, he would have nothing to remind him of Harry.

Dell showed us the only photo he has of Harry. It was taken in Hawaii on a vacation to Maui. They are both nude on a deserted beach, showing off their semi-erections. They had just made love in the ocean. They looked extremely happy. A gay pool boy offered to take the photo. Dell has his arm around Harry's neck. He is kissing Harry's head of blond hair.

TREVOR'S SURPRISE

Trevor's voice on our answering machine was a total surprise. Short and sweet, it was pure Trevor. "Hey, Miles and Abbey, this is Trevor and Gary. We and the cats, Your Highness, and Miss Missy, invite you for an Indian feast at Cambridge House, this Saturday, at six o'clock. Please bring Indian beer and your good will. Love, Trevor."

It had been over a year since that awkward rupture in our relationship that had gnawed at my conscience daily. I was nervous he would berate me, rightfully so, and I was hopeful he would somehow find the generosity to forgive us and put bygones in the past. But why should he be so generous? I deserved his wrath. I was a wreck drifting between the two outcomes. I just wanted to hold him and cry.

Gary and the cats answered the apartment door. They put us both at ease. Gary's own nervous stutter was nothing compared to mine. Abbey gave Gary a warm hug. I completely forgot what I had planned to say. I was momentarily speechless. Trevor stepped forward and simply hugged us together in silence as I started to cry. "Dear God, I have missed you. Please forgive me." "That is all right, I have already forgiven you both long ago. Thank you for coming." I could see Trevor desperately wanted a return to our comfortable relationship of the past, it's easy give and take, its off-color humor, it's non-judgmental air.

The meal was indeed grand—all takeout from the very best Indian restaurant in Greenwich Village. Ralph on Sunset Walk would have been impressed. The stove was never touched, no need to boil water. Trevor oversaw the presentation, fit to please the Queen herself in Buckingham Palace.

We told stories from 124 Sunset and Leather Flats late into the night. But I could see Trevor was over the Pines. He was more animated when he spoke of Hawaii. We told him of our long-term plans to buy our own place in the Pines Co-ops. "Sounds like you'll both be happier there." As we said goodnight, I welcomed the return of healing love between us. We promised to stay in touch. I also felt the inevitable distance between us. It was no one's fault. That closeness we discovered over two summers on Sunset and Neptune Walks, could never be recreated. It belonged to the last chapter of our childhoods. Those summers were our adolescent years, compressed in time. It truly seems all gay men are late bloomers.

KYOTO

Two years into my HIV+ status, my health was still reasonable, but Abbey and I felt like we were living in three-month installments. I got my blood drawn every three months to track my T-cell count. The lab numbers bounced around. My doctors told me that was normal. Waiting for the lab results was always very stressful. We felt like the bottom could fall out at any moment. Death was all around us. We'd attend memorial services for friends who had died of AIDS. They were invariably grim affairs, always ending the same way with lots of hugs and tears. I could see the visible strain on Abbey. My heart would break anew each time I held him in my arms. These were the most difficult times.

It felt like we needed a serious distraction. I had always wanted to see "old" Japan. It seemed like it was now or never. I proposed Kyoto for the entire month of October. Abbey agreed. No tour group, just the two of us with a few serious guide books. A real romantic adventure. We'd skip congested Tokyo all together, fly in and out of Osaka. Just do old Kyoto, Japan's original capital, with its ancient wooden buildings. Let it soak in. Stay in a traditional Japanese ryokan with futons, tatami mats, shoji screens and, yes, a wooden soaking tub. We could take in all the Japanese gardens with autumn's red maple trees, tour the ancient wooden temples with their massive bells for daily prayer, eat sushi with the locals. We were totally psyched. Door-to-door, the whole trip took twenty-four hours. Once we got there, it was like we had landed on another planet. Everything was strange, but exquisite, beautiful, perfect.

We arrived early for our morning appointment to see Saiho-ji, the Moss Temple, in the countryside outside of Kyoto. The taxi ride from our ryokan took almost an hour. A friend in New York City had forewarned us to make reservations months in advance from the States. On the way in, our small tour group of about half a dozen people, first stopped in the Founder's Hall for a brief meditation ceremony intended to empty our minds of worldly thoughts before entering the garden. There was lots of soothing chanting, with incense and bells. We were each handed a tiny paper scroll and a pencil to write a "wish." The scrolls were then collected by a priest and placed inside a huge ceramic urn to be blessed.

Entering the large four-acre garden, our first impression was of a quiet deeply forested place with a dark, yet gleaming sheet of water. Walking along the path, we noticed that soft moss, in many different shades of green, covered every surface. It was super quiet. The moss carpet absorbed all sound. The large pond had several islands joined by traditional Japanese arched bridges with rock outcroppings. Mottled lichens covered the rocks and tree trunks; brilliant red maples contrasted with the green moss carpet. There was a soothing softness to all the surfaces that was very pleasant. When we finally departed several hours later, we discovered all the return taxis were long gone. No problem, a country tea house nearby called a taxi for us and gave us tea and biscuits while we waited.

Decades later we told each other our hand written "wishes" on the paper scrolls. They were much too private to have revealed to each other back in the Moss Temple. Abbey had wished I would survive AIDS and I had wished that Abbey would find future happiness for himself if I were to die of AIDS.

WINTER PILGRIMAGE

I'm always partial to winter's light; it seems the most flattering. Summer light is much too intense and spring light is temperamental. Autumn's light is superb when it chooses to be, but that may be too infrequent. It was late winter, early March 1991. Abbey and I were on a pilgrimage to the Co-ops. Just for a few brief hours at mid-day inside the Co-op duplex rental. Enough to feed the soul until we returned every weekend in just three weeks starting on Memorial Day.

Only the hard-core were huddled in the small enclosure of the Sayville ferry boat. Ralph and Murray, John Laub and Bruce, a few contractors, Walter and Joyce who own the Pines Hardware Store, a few realtors with their clients out house shopping. A skeletal staff would open the Pines Pantry from ten to two. If you were lucky, they'd prepare their breaded chicken cutlet sandwich for you on a Keiser roll. But it was clear, it was still the off season. There were few boats in the Pines marina. Boardwalks in the shade still had a bit of snow covering them. The mourning doves were strangely missing. Without their heart-breaking call, the Pines was not herself.

"How are you boys? It's wonderful to see you both. I heard the good news from Murray. Congratulations on your skillful negotiations with Mandy. He's impossible." That was David, Ray and Murray's other law partner. David likes me for some unknown reason. He's always looking out for me. I think of him as a father. I really love him. "We'll have you and Abbey over for dinner as soon as the Co-ops open. That's Memorial Day weekend, right? We always look back fondly on our years of living in the Co-ops. In many ways, Frank and I were happier there than in our giant house on Teal. It was very social. Take care of yourself Miles. Nice to see you both."

They were using the small boat. It's tiny compared to the Clipper. The super-cute cabin boy who mans the ropes wasn't out yet. I wasn't the only one to be disappointed. He's always a pleasant sight in his dirty Levi's, his cute butt on display. As we pulled into the Pines harbor I felt an adrenalin rush. We were home.

The Co-ops looked splendid in the mid-day sun; their pitched white roofs full of welcoming glass. Since the Co-ops are right in the center of the harbor, it was only a minute walk to our unit. Abbey ran ahead. The red spiral staircase welcomed us up to our future duplex. Wow! The south facing deck was warm from the strong sun. Abbey opened the glass slider and stepped inside. "This is terribly exciting Miles. Give us a kiss." I did a lot more than just that. "Come here, my stud. You need to be serviced properly in our new home. Get that butt over here." We made love on the Ultrasuede sofa in the sun. I felt like a porno star, strong and virile. Abbey was driving me crazy. Afterwards, I just lay in Abbey's arms, the happiest man in the world. At that special moment, I had it all, my true love Abbey, my good health, my satisfying work as an architect and now our new home in the Pines. I was a very happy man indeed.

Season Four
1991

FOURTH CALLING

The fourth phone call came from Alton, Illinois.

It was Rich's mom.
I'm afraid she was weeping.
She wrote Rich a letter every day for twenty-two years.
Sweet Rich passed away overnight in his pajamas.
Rich was a mamas' boy. He was never any trouble at all.
The funeral will take place in Alton. He loved that little town.

God, this isn't right.
Rich deserves sainthood.
He loved his brothers, everyone.
Jim and Philip will welcome Rich to heaven.

We spent lazy afternoons on the grass at the Cornell Plantations.
Just slow kissing, nothing more. The orange Porsch was always spotless.

Harken you band of cheerful Angels. Look sharp!
Sir Richard is ready for his ascension to heaven.

A SLICE OF HEAVEN

It must have been our reward for being so patient. It was the start of our fourth season in the Pines. We knew from the first season that we weren't really cut out to be house mothers taking care of others. We were both too self-centered and controlling for that. The Co-ops were more where we belonged. Independent, but not isolated. The Co-ops were the right balance. The two-bedroom duplex apartment was all that we desired. I wondered what David meant when he said he and Frank were the happiest when they lived in the Co-ops. He said, "It was social." I already sensed that was at the heart of it. It was sort of like a hippie commune with free love flowing everywhere you turned. The way Dell welcomed us into his life, the way he shared his precious memories of Harry with us. Of course, Dell forced himself into our bed. As the respected elder, we understood he was partially entitled. We certainly never complained. He was a sexy passionate lover. He spoiled us with his erotic energy, his genuine affection and love. But he always made certain to love us equally. Dell was not there to question our relationship. He knew that was our rock, solid and secure. During that first month, the three of us slept together several times. When it lost its magic, we all agreed it was time to quit. It was our silent way of bonding.

Our upstairs neighbor Tommy was another story altogether. He lived alone like a hermit. His occasional Latin boyfriend Roberto, dropped by on Sundays to share the Sunday *New York Times*. Tommy was a competitive Olympic gymnast in his youth. He was still in great shape. He had a set of professional ropes hanging from his living room cathedral ceiling. Every afternoon he'd practice for an hour. I could spy on him from a jalousie window in our downstairs bedroom. I sensed he knew I was watching and didn't care in the least. He was extremely graceful, flying effortlessly through the air. I was completely mesmerized. He looked like a God in his white tights. We never spoke about it. It was much too private.

Downstairs in the garden apartment next to Dell was the long-established couple, Dave and Richard. Dave was the Co-op's accountant, a real bean counter. He made sure they were in good shape financially. Richard was a bank accountant. They'd been together for ages, but lived apart in separate apartments in the West Village. They were extremely close to Dell. Everything was a routine with them. Without fail every Friday night after dinner, they always watched *The Women*. They could quote us any line. Autumn they always vacationed in Paris, staying at the same small hotel on Ile Saint-Louis. They had their favorite bakery for breakfast croissants and their favorite French restaurant for dinner. This went on-and-on for decades.

Overall, the Co-op residents were colorful. They included a famous fashion designer in a star building, our friends Nick the CPA and Jeremy the architect in the studios and retired John and Sam in the front row facing the Atlantic Ocean. Altogether the Co-ops had a hundred units in a broad mix of gay men. They mostly kept to themselves. We also had an outrageous lesbian couple, as well as several straight couples to round things out a bit.

The grounds were popular for late-night cruising. In the daytime the same grounds were a social scene that never fully abated. Everybody knew each other's business, and they were either good old friends or ex-lovers. If they didn't meet either of those categories, they were either antisocial misfits or sex addicts who lived in the Meat Rack. Trevor's friend Saul matched both those categories. During daylight hours Saul slept in his studio apartment. After dark you could find him in the Rack.

The largest unit in the Co-ops belonged to two gay brothers, the Roberts. They were wealthy stock brokers. They owned a pair of adjacent duplex units which they combined creating East Roberts and West Roberts. Dell knew them well. He arranged to have Abbey and me meet them at their mid-summer house party which highlighted the display of their vast collection of owls. At the party we met their good friend Arthur, a prominent Hollywood screenwriter.

We enjoyed the feisty independent men of the Co-ops, like the ex-Marine Sarge. He was a nudist with the nickname "Kayak Katie." He'd row out into international waters in his kayak to converse with the Russian fishermen. Trim Sarge and the overweight Co-op Treasurer Rob had a running feud that went back decades. Whenever Sarge crossed paths with Rob, he would yell out, "Suck in that gut, Soldier!"

The Co-op rental was a success. There were no problems. We told Candy to proceed with the purchase. Dell toasted us with a bottle of champaign.

AMFAR

I was terribly proud when Abbey decided to quit his job in the Asian import business and join the American Foundation for AIDS Research (AmFAR). It was the leading national organization started in 1985 by Elizabeth Taylor and Dr. Mathilde Krim to support research in the fight against AIDS. Abbey would be their grants administrator for a decade. He was tired of watching friends die while patiently waiting for treatment options. He and other persons like him, created hope for HIV+ people like me. To date, AmFAR has invested over $617 million in its programs and has awarded more than 3,300 grants to research teams worldwide. Not a day went by that I didn't appreciate the selfless work these folks did. Abbey would often come home late exhausted from the work on the front lines. Later Abbey would look back on it as the most rewarding work of his career in the not-for-profit sector.

Of course gay men always know how to party. AmFAR, was sometimes known as GlamFAR, for its glamorous fund-raising events that featured Hollywood super-stars and artists in the entertainment industries like Madonna and hundreds of others. Abbey would tell me how Elizabeth Taylor would occasionally visit the office, telling the boys dirty jokes to cheer them on, while asking them what urgent projects needed funding.

FIFTH CALLING

The fifth phone call came from Rothstein, Logan, Lincoln and
Goldberg.

It was Murray.
He sounded exhausted.
Ray died peacefully in his sleep,
with a morphine drip as prearranged.
His last feeble words were saved for Trevor,
via a phone call through a hospice aide.

Ray was a butch Texan,
tough as steel, through and through.
He played rough with the leather boys,
with a heart of gold showing through.

You wouldn't want to face off with Ray in a courtroom.
He cut his adversaries into a million shreds.

Harken you docile Angels.
Ray already has your number.

Season Five
1992

PUSSY WILLOW

We wanted our Co-op closing to take place at the beach rather than in a Manhattan law office. No one objected. It seemed especially fitting. Murray was our attorney. Of course, Mandy didn't show up. Mac was kind enough to sit in for Mandy pro bono. Afterwards, Abbey and I took everyone out to lunch at the Blue Whale. It was the least we could do. We never could have done it all on our own. It was a community undertaking. We sensed a general sigh of relief. Mandy had no friends left in the Pines. Harry, looking down from heaven, must have been the only one to shed a tear for his former lover Mandy, now the community outcast. It was a lesson for all to learn from.

Years ago Harry renovated the duplex with his Pines buddy Gerald, a Pines decorator. Remember Gerald? He was the guy who seduced boys headed to the Meat Rack who fell into the swamp next to his house. Gerald was delighted to learn that we planned to restore the original design that Harry and he designed together more than a decade earlier. The work required was mostly cosmetic.

Two original skylights in the two bedrooms were cracking and needed replacement. The Halston Ultrasuede cushions in the living room had cigarette burns and were fading from the sun exposure. The kitchen and bath were fine after a good cleaning. The Saarinen dining table and caned Breuer dining chairs needed TLC. Gerald's floating staircase that everyone loved the most was in excellent condition. The wall-to-wall industrial carpeting, which also ran up the walls behind the beds, looked fine after a careful steam cleaning. Of course, the entire unit required a fresh coat of paint throughout which I insisted on doing myself. Gerald had personally chosen the color, a soft dove gray with the subtlest hint of lavender. It was a very sophisticated color, that changed all the time depending on the light source. Sometimes it was pinkish, other times it looked a tad green, or the subtlest shade of a purple gray, or the cool gray at dawn, like in a George Inness landscape. We never tired of looking at it. Gerald retrieved the paint formula in his files. It was Pussy Willow 2752 PPG Pittsburg Paints. It was surely the most beautiful paint in the world.

Gerald had specified a color scheme of dove gray and burgundy throughout the apartment. Walls were all to be the dove gray Pussy Willow. That unified the space and made it look even larger. Bedspreads, towels and linens were by Ralph Lauren. All were in a rich burgundy. New burgundy Halston Ultrasuede sofa cushions, with elaborate Turkish corners, were specified by Gerald to match the original. The gigantic L-shaped sofa cost a small fortune. When finished it was our favorite place for relaxing in each other's arms. The cantilevered, floating seventies-look for the sofa, staircase and beds was still fresh and elegant. All the lighting was recessed on dimmers. At night the space was dreamy. We added blue onyx tops for a pair of custom steel side tables which I designed. Gerald was pleased. When we were done, all agreed, it was the most beautiful apartment in the Co-ops. It exceeded Gerald's expectations. The decorator inside him smiled.

COMING OUT AGAIN

I soon discovered that being HIV positive was going to force me to come out all over again, whether I wanted to or not. I would have to decide who to tell or not. Initially, I felt terribly isolated. I told Abbey I wanted to tell all my friends. He cautioned restraint in light of the AIDS phobia that was widespread at the time. Could I really be denied health insurance or lose my job? What about access to the gym or a restaurant? It went far beyond practicing safe sex. I felt like "damaged goods." I shouldn't touch other people. During those years HIV positive men like me were very paranoid.

I explained to Abbey I needed to be open to friends, otherwise how could I accept their love and support that I desperately needed? We argued about this issue more than any other issue we had ever faced together. I was not consistent. I readily admitted I was HIV+, but I refused to admit I had AIDS as long as my T-cell count was over 200. That was the widely accepted guideline. The truth was, I have never had a T-cell count below 400 in the thirty-five years I have been HIV+. I was never hospitalized. I never had an opportunistic infection. I used these facts as my primary line of defense, "See, I'm healthy. I will not get sick. I don't have AIDS." Yes and no. Finally, I broke down and started crying.

I told Abbey I couldn't take the lies and deception any longer. It was too suffocating, it was unbearable, I missed my brothers, my network of support. Abbey finally got it. He hugged me. We wept together. "Fine Miles. I will support you a hundred per cent. You are very brave." This tear-drenched scene repeated itself over and over again a hundred times. Coming out as a gay man who is HIV+. It still goes on today. It never gets any easier. I always feel like I'm jumping off a cliff. But the truth is, the person on the other end has never let me down. I always get their love, especially the unconditional love from Abbey. It feels wonderful. Without their love I would have died a hundred deaths.

THE CLUB

Dell knew everyone, that is, everyone worth knowing. He was egalitarian about it; the cabin boy on the Sayville ferry or the billionaire David Geffen in his ocean-front home designed by Charles Gwathmey. They were treated equally, with respect and love. Good looks, good jokes, or an extra-large cock got you in the door, on the invite list, maybe even on the A team. Dell was all of the above. Dell was at all the hottest parties in the Pines, the ninety-year-old twinkie, the elder hustler who knew how to charm your pants off. Dell was a card-carrying member of the Club.

It was four-thirty, low tea at the Blue Whale. Abbey and I were hanging out on the front deck with Dell, just taking in the vibe, with disco on the stereo, cruising the cute Porto Rican kids dancing in their skimpy torn Levi's. Off to the side was a buffed middle-aged bronzed deity, in his perfect baseball cap, his perfect ironed chinos, his perfect white Calvin Klein tee. The guy waves across the dance floor to Dell. Abbey asks, "Who is that?" "Come with me boys. I need to introduce you to someone." Standing in front of the total stranger, Dell makes the introductions. "Hello David darling, these are my dear friends, Abbey and Miles." "A pleasure to meet you both. You make a sexy couple." That was David, David Geffen, probably the richest gay man in the world. And to think we just shook hands. That was the Pines. It was egalitarian.

Dell's closest Pines buddies made up a quartet. Their friendship went back many decades. Besides the eldest Dell, it included the decorator Gerald and the long-established couple Frank and David. Frank was a dentist whose clients were mostly gay men of the Pines. David was the Logan in the Manhattan law firm Rothstein, Logan, Lincoln and Goldberg. We met David way back at that interview for 124 Sunset with Murray and Ralph. David had poked his head into the conference room to say hello. I remember the strange feeling, like we'd already met somewhere. He shook my hand, holding it as he looked in my eyes. David was always super-friendly. Shortly after our Co-op closing he and Frank had us over on Teal Walk for a barbeque dinner and a night swim in their pool.

That's when it all came together. "Remember our encounter in Man's Country?" Suddenly, I recalled the whole thing vividly. It was a few years back on a snowy night. Abbey was away somewhere for AmFAR. I went to Man's Country alone. I peeked in an open door where an attractive man was lying on his stomach. He had the most beautiful butt I'd ever seen. I went inside and gently closed the door. I just rested my hand on his butt petting it slowly for the longest time. I could have kept my hand there forever. He looked around to give me a warm smile. "Hello. I'm David." We had the most intense sex without speaking a word. Afterwards, we exchanged numbers, but I never called him. I knew we were both in relationships. Our encounter was just meant to be a one-time thing. David became my second father. He gave me free legal advice when I needed it the most. Now, when the quartet would meet up in Dell's apartment downstairs for simple Friday night dinners, I would listen for David's gentle voice, always soft and soothing. I'd think back on that snowy night in Man's Country, the special night when we both went wild.

Sixth Calling

The sixth phone call came from Manhasset, Long Island.

It was Simon's brother Charlie.
He sounded quite depressed.
Simon died overnight at St. Vincent's.
He had wasted away to a mere skeleton.
Simon wanted Miles to have the Harley.
Sell everything else and give the proceeds to AmFAR.

Charlie hardly knew Simon.
Their paths never really crossed.
Simon wants his ashes scattered,
in the Meat Rack on Fire Island Pines.

Simon gave me a private tour of Pier 52.
We made love in the sunlight, surrounded by his brothers.

Harken you Angels of the Night.
Simon is on the Harley, riding the beach alone, the stars are overhead.

Hands On

Nick and Jeremy called up. They missed us. How about an early Saturday supper and then a session of hands-on healing? I had a flashback to that hot Labor Day orgy we enjoyed so much with Nick and Jeremy on the floor. Jeremy is really into that stuff, but I had some big news of my own I had to get out. I was a nervous wreck. I couldn't wait any longer, so I pulled everyone unto the floor and just jumped in. "We got our test results last week and I'm HIV positive, Abbey is HIV negative. My T-cells are over 650 which is the good news. I have a great new AIDS doc that Abbey found." Dead silence.

Oh my God, I've freaked them out. Now what? Jeremy broke the ice for me and made it easy. He slowly stood up and picked my armpits off the floor from behind, holding me limp in his embrace. I closed my eyes and let him take control. He gently lowered my upper body back down to the floor with my back on pillows. He gently pulled off my t-shirt and gym shorts. Then he slowly massaged my entire body with baby oil from head to toe. Jeremy had me completely relaxed. I fell asleep. When I awoke a large warm pool of cum was all over my chest. I felt absolutely wonderful.

"Wow! That was awesome, just like my first wet dream as a boy. Thank you Jeremey. I'll be back for more!" We all enjoyed a good laugh. I felt calm for the first time in weeks. What a breakthrough! I got the message. It was all right that I was HIV+. I started crying. Jeremy gave me the best hug. Jeremy spoke to me from his heart. "It's okay Miles, we all love you. We can help you get through this challenge. Just remember, at all moments in your life, awake or asleep, you are not alone. We are at your side."

SEASON SIX
1993

MOTHER'S WEEK III

This year Mother's Week took place in our new duplex in the Co-ops. The renovation was complete, so the place looked its best. Shirley and Terry each had their own bedroom. We slept at Nick and Jeremy's. Of course, Dell was out all week. He behaved himself, no lounging around in his underwear on his front deck. Actually, Dell was very sweet and made a lasagna Wednesday night.

The girls made a few new friends dancing at the Blue Whale. Since they liked it so much, we suggested a late night out at the Pavilion. We gave them ear plugs and we all took naps before heading over at midnight. When the DJ realized they were our moms, he played their requests. Judy Garland for Shirley and Frank Sinatra for Terry. There was no shortage of Pines men who wanted to dance with them. It was a big hit. They all had a ball. We left at 2 am and slept in the next day. They wanted to buy us a housewarming gift together. We settled on Ralph Lauren bedsheets, in burgundy of course.

We surprised them with our wedding plans for next spring. They were both so proud of us. We were touched.

SUNKEN FOREST

Stan offered to take Abbey and me boating Saturday morning. He owns a small speed boat that he keeps parked in the Pines Harbor. It's his boy toy. If you asked me, I'd say it's just a headache, taking it in and out of the water each season, plus constant cleaning and waxing. But it's not my boat. Stan seems to really enjoy it.

I suggested he take us to Sunken Forest; Stan had never been. It's within the Fire Island National Seashore, facing the Great South Bay, about two miles west of the Pines. Abbey and I walked there once a few years ago. It's beautiful. It's located down behind the dunes, directly west of Sailor's Haven. Gnarled holly, sassafras, tupelo and shadblow form the canopy. Vines of catbrier, poison ivy and wild grape climb from the forest floor toward the sun. The raised boardwalk makes a giant loop, great for walking. Stan wanted to race, but Abbey pointed out the loose sand. "It's way too dangerous. You'll slide and fall." So we settled for speed walking, working up a good sweat.

"I like to see you boys get nice and sweaty. It's good for an old man like me. It makes me hard, if you know what I mean." "We hear you Stan, loud and clear. This is the Pines. Perhaps a little something can be arranged, either here or back in your hot tub. The Visitor's Center at the far end has a popular tearoom, if you're into that sort of thing." Stan said he definitely preferred the comforts of home. We agreed.

Back in the hot tub, we all took our time. Stan was feeling super horny. After a marathon session, we were all exhausted, so we napped a while on cushy deck chairs. When George finally showed up in his Speedos, we gladly indulged him in a second round. Ah, languid afternoon sex in the Pines with the mourning doves cooing in the background. Just close your eyes and let go.

SEASON SEVEN
1994

THOMAS

Midway was our favorite walk in the Pines. It ran east west at the midpoint between the bay and the ocean, from Beach Hill to Pine Walks. Because it was not a thru walk, it was extra quiet. It also had several of the grandest gardens in the Pines. The lot with the giant A-frame belonged to Thomas and Stanley, two Black doctors who were also handsome body builders. We'd take Midway just to get a glimpse of Thomas and Stanley working in their garden, shirtless in boxer trunks. On one walk-thru Murray stopped to introduce us to Thomas and Stanley. They were very friendly. When they learned I was an architect, they invited us in for a tour. It was a classic A-frame with full glass at both ends. When you were inside looking out, all you saw were the lush gardens.

Thomas pulled Abbey aside and asked if we'd be up for a foursome sometime. "I get the feeling you guys might be interested, right? I've seen you two looking in when we're in the garden." "You bet. But you should know up front, Miles is HIV+." "Well, so am I. We can still have fun with safe sex, right?" When Abbey told me this I was thrilled. "Count me in. I'm flattered." We became closest buddies. Thomas was the perfect playmate. Always safe and loving, creative and fun. He made it okay to be HIV+.

PINES HARDWARE

The quality of a community's hardware store tells you a lot about that community. The Pines had the most amazing hardware store I'd ever seen. It wasn't large, but it was extremely well stocked and organized. It was in the Pines Harbor, tucked in next to the Pines Pantry directly off Bay Walk. Of course, it was owned by a straight German couple, Walter and Joyce. Over the years of home ownership in half a dozen houses, I've noticed that Germans understand this topic better than the rest of us.

I mean, where else on earth could you find a frosted seven-watt picture tube light bulb? Or closed-cell adhesive weather-stripping in two dozen shapes, sizes and colors? And don't forget, we are talking about a store in a remote beach community, on a sandbar with no roads, surrounded by corrosive salt air from the Atlantic Ocean. It was a reflection of that community's wealth and high standards for quality. We were completely spoiled. Of course, gay men generally know a good bit about the subject of hardware. After all, isn't it our favorite topic of conversation? God bless Walter and Joyce, they always supplied us fussy queens with exactly what we asked for. You couldn't do any better than that, both in life or in the hardware store.

GETTING DOWN
TO BUSINESS

The Pines Business District consisted of some two-dozen businesses in half a dozen buildings on the west side of the Pines Harbor. It wasn't exactly like shopping on Fifth Avenue in Manhattan or even Bleeker Street in Greenwich Village. But it covered all the bases nicely for a seasonal beach community. What made it so special was the gay factor: wealthy, queer and in your face. For the Pines shopper always dressed casual in their favorite Speedos. Shopping and sex went hand-in-hand in the Pines. Whether it was buying dinner for the house in the Pines Pantry and Peter's Meat Market, picking up libations at Spirit of the Pines or Pines Liquor, or a dozen white lilies for the dinner table from the Pines Florist; you could always get someone's number along the way.

All these essential transactions could be easily concluded in the Pines Business District on your AmEx card. If you were someone's guest, you would need a thank you gift from the Crow's Nest, above the ice cream stand. If you needed something more sophisticated, check out the white-on-white selection at Wolf & Wolf. If you were staying at the Botel, poor baby, looking for true love, pick up a selection of trusty Trojan condoms in the Pines Pantry. For that party on Saturday afternoon, don't forget the colored helium balloons that Jerry and Jery are holding for you at the Crow's Nest. They also have the full selection of the latest colored jock straps, including that yellow one you have your eye on. Perfect to wear around the pool. Maybe we can take in a break upstairs at Crew's Quarters before your late afternoon meeting with our realtor Bob Howard. He has an ocean front we really should see before it goes. And don't forget to take a nap, at least two hours. We are doing the Pavilion after a midnight dinner at the Blue Whale. Michael Jorba is tonight's D.J. Can't miss that, right? Plus, we'll want to catch the sunrise.

SEASON EIGHT
1995

ALEX

Alex was my AIDS doctor for over six years between 1992 and 1998. These were the critical years where we were flying blind. AZT was the only approved drug to fight AIDS and it didn't work for most people, including me. It gave me headaches and nausea. Abbey found Alex through AmFAR. He was one of four extraordinary doctors in an AIDS practice based in Manhattan who used the latest research to find creative ways to fight the virus. Alex was like a general fighting a huge battle in the dark with very few weapons and no troops. We would try the latest experimental drugs like underground ddC from Canada. By 1995 he realized that unheard of combinations of these drugs could buy HIV+ patients time, until new stronger drugs appeared.

Every three months I saw Alex. He always recommended something new, like the combination of 3TC with d4T. I was always game for anything. My T-cells were bouncing around, up and down. The big hit for me was Viracept in mid-1998. A homerun! My T-cell count jumped up to 850, a personal all-time high. By then I was out of the woods. Alex had saved my life. He told me I could leave his practice for care with other AIDS doctors working successfully with new drugs in the AIDS arsenal. Alex had greater callings to address. I thanked him with a hand written note and a hug. I was one of the lucky ones.

By 1996, triple-drug combination therapies were being approved. Finally, we could really fight the virus by keeping the viral load down to undetectable. Abbey helped me maintain a positive attitude. I was lucky to have quality friends who knew how to best support me.

GMHC had safe sex workshops, plus nutrition and yoga classes. I could volunteer to deliver food packages to shut-ins after work. Gyms had buddies to workout with. There were even clean, well-run J.O. clubs where hot safe sex was enforced and a guy like me could still have a little fun with his brothers. The gay community was strong back then. Everybody felt connected. We understood that we were all in this mess together.

Seventh Calling

The seventh phone call came from Rothstein, Logan, Lincoln and Goldberg.

It was Murray.
He's a total wreck.
David died overnight.
It was an aggressive brain tumor.
It was inoperable.
David asked Murray to tell me he loved me.

Murray never knew this.
Frank never knew it either.
David always kept me his big secret.
I told Abbey everything from the beginning.

David and I met in Man's Country on a snowy night.
We saw the stars of heaven together. David led the way.

Harken you unsuspecting Angels.
David will wait for Miles. He is in no hurry.

CROSS DRESSER

When Rich called out of the blue, I was surprised. But when he said he wanted to visit us in the Pines, I was doubly curious. At Cornell Rich had always been closeted. I suspected he always wore facial makeup. He never asked me into his apartment in Collegetown. When I honked outside his building to give him a ride to class, he always took at least twenty minutes to appear. Was he taking off the makeup or was he getting out of a dress? Who knew?

Well, that was all cleared up when he stepped off the ferry Saturday morning in the Pines Harbor wearing a comfortable garden dress fit for the likes of Doris Day herself. Now her makeup was less subtle than what I'd seen at Cornell. Her lipstick was red, cherry red, with heavy eyeliner. She had come out big time. She was alone. The boyfriend she mentioned in passing a decade ago was no longer. She appeared to be a free woman in search of her man. No way she's a dyke. She poked fun at herself constantly, which I took as a good sign. "Aren't I a dishy queen?" Her transformation was so extreme, there was no point in asking for the play-by-play. She was simply "reborn." She now goes by Ricci rather than boring Rich. She's liberal with the French cologne. Is that Chanel No. 5?

Ricci stayed the weekend. She belted out Judy Garland torch songs karaoke-style in Crew's Quarters to an adoring crowd. Later into the night she was a big hit slow dancing up close with the big boys in the Pavilion—squeezing their butts, rubbing their cocks. She was a loose woman. She brought back Mr. Right to the Co-ops Saturday night, and caused quite a ruckus, until Dell discovered her and whisked her away for an early breakfast in bed. By Sunday afternoon she had us all exhausted. Next time, I suggested she look into the Belvedere in Cherry Grove. It might be a better fit.

SEASON NINE
1996

MEL AND DAN

My twin sister Mel and her husband Dan came for a visit on the July 4th weekend. Abbey and I proposed the Pines. They'd been there once before when we lived in Leather Flats. This would be the first time in the Co-ops. It was also the first time we hired a limousine to get us all to the Sayville ferry landing from Manhattan. They were sure impressed. It wasn't much more than four fares on the Long Island Railroad. Mel is really into gay men. She likes to flirt, to tell dirty jokes, to make them laugh. Of course, they love the attention. She's cool about gay sex, which is pretty amazing since we both grew up in a repressed Catholic family. But being twins always brought us together. Dan is a high school coach so he's very together about gay boys and their issues around team sports like football. Abbey is perfect around both of them telling jokes, doing impersonations, and generally clowning around.

When we arrived at the duplex, Dell was there to welcome us. He can be extremely charming. He started giving out neck massages. He had Mel won over immediately. "You know Mel, I have a crush on your twin Miles. Everybody does. What's his greatest secret from childhood?" "Oh that's easy. Miles always preferred boys. He played with his wee wee. He also fainted in church during Sunday Mass. He said that was because he was Saint Sebastian."

Abbey grilled his swordfish steaks and we walked to Water Island. Mostly we just talked about our hopes and our fears. They both know I'm HIV positive and Abbey is HIV negative. Mel thanked Abbey for taking such good care of her twin. She made us all cry.

EIGHTH CALLING

The eighth phone call came from the Beresford in Manhattan.

It was Gerald.
He was a total wreck.
Dell died peacefully in his sleep.
Actually, Dell was jerking off, watching porno.
It was his favorite Al Parker video.
The one where Parker fucks Casey Donovan.

Dell guarded the Nazi prisoners in WWII.
They were mostly just cute teenage boys.
Dell opened the gate to transgress them.
But he mussed their blond hair instead.

Dell always treats the boys like his children.
He sleeps in the middle forming a pile of puppies.

Harken you clever Angels.
Pay attention, Dell is watching you.

NINTH CALLING

The ninth phone call came from Hyde Park, New York.

It was Carl.
Dave killed himself.
He drank a quart of gin,
tied a rope around his neck,
then threw himself overboard his sailboat.
He sank into the turquoise-blue waters of the Bahamas.

Bob looked down in horror.
Dave had always blamed Bob for his AIDS.
Dave never heard the music; he never saw the sunrise.
Bob would be welcomed into heaven.

Abbey and I spent that final afternoon skating on the pond.
Bob cut wood with his chainsaw. Dave drank gin from his pocket flask.

Harken you lazy Devils. Wake up you ugly wretches!
Dave is finally good and ready for his descent into Hell.

SEASON TEN
1997

A FORK
IN THE ROAD

After fourteen years of summering in the Pines, I felt it was time to move on. I started looking back over my life and counted sixteen homes since childhood, moving every four-and-a-half years on average. A family of nomads. At least Abbey had the Jewish excuse, wandering in the desert for forty years. I had no excuse. Was this normal? Was it healthy? What about roots, building a foundation for life? Starting a family. We couldn't see ourselves as two gay daddies. We'd freak out at the mess.

I watched as Abbey was getting burned out from AIDS. Between me and AmFAR he was consumed with AIDS every day. And I wasn't even really sick, at least not yet. Twenty-five years of living in New York City was also taking its toll. The noise, the dirt, the traffic, the crime, the homeless, the rat race. When we were in our twenties we were resilient, ready for any challenge. But at fifty, we were feeling tired, exhausted, defeated. The Pines had always been our escape. It still was, but it was losing its edge; it was no longer fresh and exciting, it was a routine like any other, only this one was very expensive and time consuming, on a sand bar waiting to be washed away in the next hurricane.

I suggested we go back in time. Return to little Ithaca. It's quiet, gorgeous, gay friendly, cheap, full of friendly hippies, international with students and faculty from all over the globe. We could find satisfying work and maybe buy a place to retire. New York City was still a bus ride away when the urge for high culture hits. Abbey surprised me. He liked the idea. It could reignite our relationship. New friends, rescue a sweet kitty, live in a real house with a yard and an outdoor grill, buy a baby grand and a boat for Lake Cayuga. Living in New York City had a high price. Was it really worth it?

We decided to look into it. I found three good job offers in a few weeks. A great first apartment until we found our future dream house. Could it work? I decided to give it my best. I would give it a trial run for three months. I moved up alone. Abbey came up on the weekends twice a month. He fell in love with Ithaca, with my used Volvo, my kitty Molly, the Ithaca Farmer's Market, my new hippy image. I retired the black leather to the back of the closet and bought a few tie-dyed tees. We fell in love all over again.

Of course, leaving the Pines was bitter sweet. We'd miss the gossip and our wonderful friends. They seemed irreplaceable. But Ithaca was full of cute new faces as well. In time it worked out just fine. The duplex in the Co-ops sold in two weeks for a record price. It got grabbed up by a single guy who loved the color pussy willow.

RECKONING

Ten seasons spent in Fire Island Pines had left an indelible impression. It felt like my ancestral home. The six-month cycle, on again, off again, gave rhythm to our lives. Each year as winter's cold slowly receded, we ached to return in the spring to the sound of the breaking waves, to the Pines men who were even more handsome than we had remembered. Familiar old faces and exciting new smiles. We craved another season living in our Speedos, dancing shirtless in the Pavilion, walking to Water Island to share intimate conversations, cruising in the Rack for another round of intoxicating sex. Yes, sex was our drug of choice. It nourished our souls. When Halloween arrived announcing our seasonal departure, it felt like punishment for the excesses of summer. Winter was for introspection. Spring always brought our resurrection.

By any accounting, Fire Island Pines was a success. It brought isolated gay men together during a harrowing health crisis, it defined us to ourselves. We arrived frightened babes, we left wise elders. Just that would have been more than enough. But the Pines was so much more. In the deepest recesses of our subconscious, the Pines was our private haven, where we all fit in, where we all belonged.

By any reckoning the Pines was a contradiction. It was neither black nor white, but decidedly gray. The Pines was both heaven and hell, love and lust, family and isolation. At each step along the way, she offered me two outstretched hands; I kissed them both equally; one came forward with the other.

At the ocean's sandy edge, at last, I found tranquility. In the Rack, under the stars, I found the power of sex. In the Pavilion, while dancing shirtless with my brothers, I found my family.

TENTH CALLING

The tenth phone call came from Heaven.

It was Bob.
He misses me.
Heaven is boring.
He wishes he was in the Pines,
specifically in the Rack making love
to the hot young kid with the cute smile.

Dave always had to be the drama queen.
He'll probably bribe his way out of Hell.
How's your sweetheart Abbey? You are such a lucky man.
Tell him that I love him. I miss his dirty jokes.

Hang in there Miles; I know you're one of the survivors.
I want to make you that salmon souffle we shared together on Neptune.

Take a break you handsome Devil.
I'm good for now, God bless you all.

TREVOR'S
RESURRECTION

After Trevor's surprise Indian feast at the Cambridge House, our relationship finally healed. But it wasn't until the Covid years and my writing, that it showed signs of new growth. I believe I shared some of my poetry. I asked for forgiveness for my clumsy betrayal. Trevor graciously gave me that. He became my principal reader. He understood me. We exchanged photographs of our days together at Sunset. Autumn walks on a deserted beach, the two of us with Abbey, wearing our leather jackets, a soothing flood of memories. But it wasn't until Rome, that we witnessed Trevor's full-blown Resurrection, his arrival on life's center stage.

It happened in Rome, 2022, as Trevor stepped out of the driver's van, into the charming cobblestone square with its fountain. I had arranged for Trevor to stay on Via Coronari, the Renaissance street with its antique shops across from San Salvatore in Lauro. As Trevor arrived a street musician was singing Verdi opera. At first we didn't recognize him, so much time was compressed in that moment, thirty-three years. Then I recalled the hesitant smile. It was Trevor for certain.

Trevor would be in Rome for one week. The apartment was small and quirky, practicably unlivable. Trevor couldn't care in the least. His face was radiant. It was superb; Trevor's first trip to Rome, the Eternal City and I was to be his personal guide. A dozen of Rome's finest Baroque churches: Santa Maria della Pace, the Maddalena, Borromini's masterpiece Sant'Ivo, the French church San Luigi with Caravaggio's triptych of Saint Matthew in his signature red paint, its angel falling out of a black sky. I told him the stories of the artist and the saint, stories I love to share.

Baroque architecture with its colored marbles, its fat putti and its sad Madonnas welcomed us both into its mysterious fraternity of closeted priests. We both let our guard down, as we cruised the sexy young men with their black robes and their white collars. I wanted to hold your hand, to

187

muss with your hair, to make you laugh like you did back at Sunset, in the turquoise pool with your red kickboard, on that first day we met in the Pines. Soon enough our secret adventures in the Rack would bond us as brothers, brothers searching for the same thing—queer sex in the bushes, queer love in the heavens. There we were sinners and saints, if only for a week; but that week in Rome changed everything. It brought us peace and closure.

www.ingramcontent.com/pod-product-compliance
Lightning Source LLC
Chambersburg PA
CBHW010113270326
41927CB00018B/3372